The lake was beautiful, but its banks were quite steep in places, and it was deeper than the unwary might suppose. Sure enough, as Peter drew nearer, he saw a dark head bobbing just above the surface of the water. Flinging himself from the saddle, he ran the last few steps, shedding his coat and waistcoat and tossing them aside as he slid down the bank.

"Susannah, I'm coming! I'm—"

She turned at the sound of his voice, and the words died on his lips. Far from drowning, she stood at a depth of about four feet, her head and shoulders breaking the surface of the lake. Streams of water ran from her hair, trembling in diamond-like drops from the ends of each curl, spilling over bare shoulders, and running in rivulets down the slight indentation that narrowed into the crevice between her—

Crimson faced, Peter fixed his gaze determinedly on her face. "What the devil are you doing?" His breath came in laboured gasps that had little to do with his recent exertions.

"I'm taking a bath," she explained, as if bathing naked in an ornamental lake were the most natural thing in the world.

"Are you aware that the whole household is searching for you?" he demanded with less than perfect truth. "Come out of there at once! No, wait! Don't!"

Baroness

in

Buckskin

A Regency Romance

Sheri Cobb South

1

More than kisses, letters mingle souls.
JOHN DONNE, *Verse Letter to Sir Henry Wotton*

*D*inner at Ramsay Hall began just as it had every evening for longer than anyone seated at the table could remember. The head of the family (at present one Richard Ramsay, the seventh baron of that name) sat in state at the head of the long table of polished walnut. The two spinster sisters of his lordship's late father—known collectively as the Aunts—had walked up from the Dower House, as was their usual habit when the weather was fine, and now flanked him, Miss Charlotte Ramsay on his right, and Miss Amelia Ramsay, the younger by two years, on his left. Ramsay Hall had no mistress at present, for Lord Ramsay at age thirty-one was still unwed, but his lordship's distant cousin Miss Jane Hawthorne (she of the classic English rose complexion, ash-blonde hair and speaking grey eyes) now occupied the place at the foot of the table, just as she had done since the declining health of his lordship's mother, Lady Ramsay, had necessitated that she delegate this task to her companion. The present arrangement was admittedly a trifle irregular, since with the death of Lady Ramsay more than a year ago, the honour of acting as hostess should have fallen to the elder of the Aunts, but Miss Charlotte Ramsay had been quite scandalized by the suggestion that she should alter in any way the routine which had been established by his lordship's dearest mama. And so Miss Hawthorne—distant cousin, poor relation, and, according to the less charitable residents of Lower Nettleby, general drudge —remained in the position rightfully belonging to the lady of the house. At Miss Hawthorne's right sat Mr. Peter Ramsay, yet another distant cousin, who at the tender age of three-and-twenty had already served as Lord Ramsay's steward for almost two years.

The conversation, too, followed a long-established pattern, first taking in everyone's opinion of the weather, and then widening in concentric circles to encompass the estate and then the village beyond. (The concerns of the wider world would be taken up by the gentlemen after the ladies had retired to the drawing room, where they would no doubt exchange their own views on this subject, on which the male contingent assumed them to be entirely ignorant.)

"Another fine day," was Lord Ramsay's opening observation, delivered as the soup was served.

"Indeed yes! If we don't have rain soon, I fear for my poor roses," fretted Miss Amelia, whose garden, besides being her consuming passion, was one of the glories of Lower Nettleby.

"Much as I regret being forced to disagree with you, Aunt Amelia, I hope the rain will hold off until the tenants' cottages can be inspected and any necessary repairs made." Young Mr. Peter Ramsay turned to address his lordship. "Jem Pittingly says the thatch on his roof needs to be replaced."

Lord Ramsay nodded. "Very well. I shall see to it in the morning." His visage was somewhat stern, but the smile he bent upon his aunt was surprisingly sweet. "After all, we cannot expect Aunt Amelia's roses to wait forever."

"Perhaps I might tell Sir Matthew that they died," she pondered wistfully. "He *will* keep badgering me for cuttings, and you may think it unchristian of me, but I do not want to share!"

Miss Hawthorne came quickly to her defense. "Naturally you do not, for you cultivated that particular color yourself, did you not? But although his entreaties may grow tedious, I do not believe there is any real harm in Sir Matthew. You have only to tell him how you feel, and I am certain you will find him understanding. On the subject of gardening, anyway," she added somewhat obscurely.

"Wise Jane!" applauded Lord Ramsay from the opposite end of the table. "I feel sure you may place every dependence on her advice, Aunt Amelia, for she has handled Sir Matthew quite adroitly for nearly a decade."

Miss Hawthorne gave him a reproachful look, but Aunt Amelia seized upon his advice. "My dear Jane, would you speak to him on my behalf? Just a subtle hint, you know."

Having assured Aunt Amelia of Sir Matthew's willingness to see reason, she could hardly demur, although she had never seen any evidence that their nearest neighbor was open to subtle hints. She agreed, albeit reluctantly, to speak to the baronet on Amelia's behalf.

"Excellent!" exclaimed her aunt, much cheered. "He is certain to listen to you, for he has the highest opinion of you."

"But not half so high as his opinion of himself," grumbled Aunt Charlotte under her breath, thereby winning a concurring smile from Miss Hawthorne.

"I see no reason why Jane should be put to the trouble of routing Sir Matthew," his lordship protested. "If he is plaguing you, Aunt Amelia, you have only to tell him that I will not allow it. He is as cautious of my position as he is his own, and will not press the matter if he believes it would offend me."

"Oh, but I could not tell so blatant a falsehood, not even in defense of my poor roses! 'Not allow it,' indeed, when you are the most good-natured boy imaginable! Why, when I think of how kind you have been to my dear sister and me, giving us the Dower House and a positively *lavish* allowance beside—"

She might have continued in this vein indefinitely, had she not been interrupted by the soft-footed entrance of Wilson, the butler, bearing a silver tray on which reposed a formerly white rectangle of paper, now much smudged and creased.

"Forgive me, my lord," he said, proffering the tray and its contents to Lord Ramsay, "but the evening post has just been delivered, and I believe your lordship has been expecting a communication from America for some time."

"America?"

A collective gasp was heard around the table. Lord Ramsay winced slightly, wishing for a bit more discretion on the part of his servant. Nevertheless, he took the missive lying on the tray and broke the wax seal, then spread the single sheet and perused its contents while his relations waited in silent expectation.

"I beg your pardon, Peter," he told his cousin, having reached the end of his correspondence. "I fear I must leave the matter of the Pittingly cottage in your capable hands. Do whatever the situation requires; I have every confidence in your judgment. I must away to London, but I shall settle any expenses you incur as soon as I return."

"To London, Richard?" asked Miss Hawthorne, speaking for the group. "I hope nothing is wrong."

"Not at all, but I must go to London to see the Archbishop about a special license." His gaze took in every member of his family at a glance, from the bewildered expressions of his elderly aunts to the perplexed look of his steward to Jane's curiously white, strained countenance. "You see, I am to be married."

A stunned silence greeted this pronouncement, broken only when Aunt Amelia exclaimed in blissful accents, "Married! A wedding at Ramsay Hall? How lovely!"

"And you are marrying an American, Richard dear?" asked Aunt Charlotte with a faint air of disapproval. "I didn't know you were acquainted with any."

A flicker of a smile lit Lord Ramsay's stern countenance. "You make it sound as if I am taking a Red Indian to wife. As it happens, my betrothed and I have never met face to face, but her birth is quite respectable. Miss Susannah Ramsay is a distant cousin, the granddaughter of Benjamin Ramsay, who was quartered in Virginia during the war against the American colonies and remained there afterwards to marry a local woman. Old Benjamin's son Gerald, Susannah's father, died recently, leaving her alone in the world."

"And so you naturally considered it your duty to offer her marriage," observed Miss Hawthorne without, she was pleased to note, a hint of irony in her voice.

"But Richard!" exclaimed Aunt Amelia, her childlike countenance crumpling as her romantic dreams died a-borning. "You cannot love her. Is this what you want, to marry a female sight unseen?"

His lordship sighed, and his gaze drifted to the portrait adorning the far wall, the bewigged likeness of the third Baron Ramsay, who had almost bankrupted the family in the South Sea Bubble of the previous century, and who had been held up to his descendants ever since as a horrible example. "I haven't the luxury of pursuing my own desires, Aunt. I myself am no more than a placeholder. It is my duty as head of this family to see to the welfare of its members, and to pass my birthright intact—and enlarged, if possible—on to the next baron. As Miss Susannah Ramsay is the sole heiress to considerable properties in both Virginia and Kentucky, I have in her person the opportunity to do both."

"Such romantic flights of fancy!" chided Miss Hawthorne with a twinkle in her eye. "Take care that you are not utterly carried away, Richard."

"I shall depend upon my practical Cousin Jane to keep my feet securely planted on the ground," promised his lordship in like manner. "In the meantime, I have booked passage for Miss Ramsay on the schooner *Concordia*, and she is to arrive in Portsmouth in six weeks' time."

"She is traveling all the way across the ocean alone?" exclaimed Aunt Charlotte, horrified. "She sounds a very ramshackle sort of female, I must say."

"I believe she is to be traveling in the company of a missionary couple, so there is nothing in the least objectionable about her undertaking such a journey." He turned to address his steward. "Peter, I shall depend on you to meet Miss Ramsay in Portsmouth and convey her to Ramsay Hall."

Peter Ramsay's fork clattered against his plate, the sound unnaturally loud in the strained silence. "Very well, Cousin Richard, if you wish it. But hadn't you better—that is, would you not prefer to meet your affianced bride yourself? Forgive me, but I cannot help but think Miss Ramsay might perceive your seeming neglect as an insult."

"I can see you have little knowledge of women, Cousin Peter, and still less of marriage." Seeing his steward's puzzled expression, he explained, "Miss Susannah Ramsay will soon be obliged to see my face over the breakfast table for the rest of her life. Surely she will welcome this brief respite."

"If she is that unwilling, Richard, perhaps she would have done better to have declined your offer," suggested Jane Hawthorne from the opposite end of the table.

"Perhaps she would, at that," Lord Ramsay concurred. "I can only hope that she is not so exacting in her requirements as certain other young ladies of my acquaintance."

Although these words were accompanied by his lordship's surprisingly sweet smile, Miss Hawthorne's cheeks burned nevertheless, and at the first opportunity, she rose from the table as the signal for the ladies to withdraw.

Alas, there was no relief in the drawing room conversation that followed.

"Well!" exclaimed Aunt Charlotte. "What do you think of *that?*"

No one was left in any doubt that "that" referred to Lord Ramsay's unexpected betrothal.

"I would feel better if I thought dear Richard could love her," fretted Aunt Amelia. "I can't help feeling that she must be a shockingly *vulgar* creature!"

"So many Americans are, you know," agreed Aunt Charlotte, who to Jane's knowledge had never met an American in her life.

"Nonsense!" Miss Hawthorne declared briskly. "I am sure I feel quite sorry for her, being obliged to leave her home and travel across the ocean to be married to a man she has never met. I am determined to be kind to her if it kills me, and I hope both of you will do the same."

The two elderly sisters exchanged uncomfortable glances, then Aunt Amelia spoke for both. "Truth to tell, Jane dear, we rather hoped you and Richard would someday make a match of it."

Miss Hawthorne greeted the arrival of the tea tray with patent relief, and busied herself with the pouring and passing of cups.

"I had my opportunity once, as you know," she said, after the footman had withdrawn and the ladies of the house were alone again. "I had no desire to be married out of a sense of duty then, and no more do I now. If Miss Susannah Ramsay's situation demands that she accept such an offer without so much as a glimpse of her prospective bridegroom, then surely she deserves our pity."

The Aunts gave her looks of silent sympathy but, thankfully, dropped the subject. Lord Ramsay and Peter joined them several minutes later, and the thoughtful frown creasing Peter's brow gave Miss Hawthorne to understand that the gentlemen's conversation had followed very similar lines. After partaking of tea with the ladies, Lord Ramsay rang for a footman to set up the card table, and he and Peter played at silver loo with the Aunts while Jane entertained them on the pianoforte. This long-established routine held until the clock struck nine, at which time his lordship turned once again to his faithful steward.

"Peter, can I entrust you to escort Aunt Charlotte and Aunt Amelia back to the Dower House? Jane, I should like a word with you, if I may."

Miss Hawthorne was uncomfortably aware of the thudding of her own heart as she bade the Aunts goodbye and followed Lord Ramsay to his study.

"Yes, Richard? What is it?"

He sighed and withdrew a folded rectangle of paper from the inside breast pocket of his coat. "I feel I owe you an explanation."

"Nonsense! You owe me nothing of the kind."

"Perhaps not, but I should feel better if you allow me to make one all the same."

She inclined her head in agreement. "Very well, then."

He handed her the paper, and she spread the single sheet. It was a letter, as she had expected, but she was surprised to note that it was not the letter that had been delivered during dinner. This one was considerably older, bearing a date some three months earlier in the upper right-hand corner, a date written in a spidery, feminine hand. It had been folded and refolded so many times that the paper was worn quite thin along the creases; however unexpected his lordship's announcement, the decision had apparently not been made without a great deal of consideration.

"The Right Honourable the Lord Ramsay," it read, "I hope you will pardon my presumption in writing to you without a proper introduction, but I fear my Christian duty demands nothing less. I wish to bring to your attention the plight of my young friend and your distant kinswoman, Miss Susannah Ramsay. Miss Ramsay's father, Mr. Gerald Ramsay, recently died after a lengthy illness, leaving Miss Ramsay alone in the world at the age of eighteen. Her situation is most uncomfortable—not that she is penniless (in fact, she is the sole heiress to a town house in Richmond as well as a large property in Kentucky), but she is sure to be the object of attentions with which I fear she is ill-prepared to cope. It would be an exaggeration to say that her father lost his wits after the death of his wife when Susannah was only two years old, but there is no denying the fact that he became quite eccentric, burying himself and his small daughter in the wilds of Kentucky. He certainly prospered there, but at the expense of Susannah's upbringing. Although she is both intelligent and kindhearted, she is in no way fit to be presented to Richmond society, and I confess I fear for her future. If you can see your way to providing for her in some way, I am sure all who care for her must be eternally grateful. Yours most sincerely, Mrs. Charles Latham."

Having reached the end of this extraordinary correspondence, Miss Hawthorne looked up at his lordship. "And so, discovering Miss Ramsay to be unsuited to Virginia society, you decided to inflict her on London society instead," she observed with a hint of a smile.

"Hardly that," protested Lord Ramsay. "I am uninterested in cutting a dash in London, so it matters little whether my wife is fashionable or not."

"Has the girl no maternal relations who might take an interest in her welfare?"

He shook his head. "According to her lawyer—Mrs. Latham's letter was enclosed with his—her mother's people cut her grandmother off during the war, when she took up with one of the despised redcoats. So Miss Ramsay can look for no help from that quarter."

"But marriage is so—so drastic. And so permanent. Can you not simply bring her here and make her an allowance instead?"

"I suppose I might," he said with a sigh, "but truth to tell, I am reluctant to take responsibility for yet another dependent female."

Miss Hawthorne flinched. "I beg your pardon, Richard. I did not know you felt that way. If you will give me a reference, I shall seek another position at once—"

"Jane!" he exclaimed in some consternation. "You cannot think I was speaking of you! No, I was thinking of Aunt Charlotte and Aunt Amelia. In fact, I am very grateful for your presence, for I have a particular favour to ask of you."

"A favour, Richard? What is it?"

He gestured toward the letter in her hand. "If Mrs. Latham is correct, Miss Ramsay, however untutored, does not lack intelligence. Which is a very good thing, as I could not bring myself to take a stupid woman to wife, however dire her circumstances! I shall depend upon you to show her how to go on, to teach her what she must know to have charge of the running of a sizeable household."

"And if she resents my meddling?"

"What meddling? You were companion to the last Lady Ramsay; why should you not be companion to the next? A suggestion here, a subtle hint there, and you will have her performing the rôle as if to the manner born. Please say you will, Jane, for I know of no other woman to whom I could entrust such a task."

She could not deny the practicality of Lord Ramsay's proposal. She had no desire to leave Ramsay Hall and seek employment elsewhere. Nor, for that matter, was anyone more qualified to instruct the next Lady Ramsay in the running of the household which Jane herself had overseen ever since the dowager's health had failed.

"Very well, Richard. I accept."

"Bless you!" he exclaimed, seizing her hand and raising it to his lips. "I knew I could depend on you, best of cousins!"

She would not disappoint him. She would take poor little Miss Ramsay under her wing and turn her into a comfortable wife for his lordship and a suitable mistress for Ramsay Hall.

And she would never give either of them reason to suspect that she had been deeply in love with Richard Ramsay for more than a decade.

2

She never told her love,
But . . . sat like Patience on a monument,
Smiling at grief.
WILLIAM SHAKESPEARE, *Twelfth Night*

*L*ooking back, Jane supposed it had been inevitable. She had been only eighteen when her father's death had left her cast adrift on the world, much as Miss Susannah Ramsay had been after the death of her own father. But whereas the late Mr. Ramsay had been a wealthy eccentric, Mr. Hawthorne had been a charming wastrel, leaving nothing behind at his death but a mountain of debts, a bevy of disconsolate mistresses, and a daughter of marriageable age with no dowry to speak of. When she had first met her cousin Richard, he was twenty-one years old and in mourning for his father, having attained his majority and come into his title within the space of a month. Upon being informed of her existence, he had lost no time in making her acquaintance, and had no sooner straightened up from his introductory bow than he had dropped to one knee and made her a formal offer of marriage.

She had not accepted, of course. Never mind the fact that she was a Ramsay only on the distaff side—and one had to go back five generations to find the common ancestor—Richard's determination to do his duty in spite of his own inclination had been so obvious that she could not have brought herself to (as he said) make him the happiest of men, no matter how dire her prospects for the future. In the end it had been Lady Ramsay, his mother, who had settled the matter by bringing Jane to Ramsay Hall as her companion. In fact, so adroit had been her ladyship's handling of the situation that it had not been long before she and Richard were able to face one another without any of the awkwardness usually attending a rejected proposal of marriage. They had soon become friends, and eventually trusted confidantes. But the damage, if it might be so described, was done: to young Jane, whose only experience of men was a father who knew no obligation but the pursuit of his own pleasure, the kindness of the youthful Lord Ramsay was irresistible. She had fallen head over ears, and the intervening years had shown her nothing in Richard's character to make her revise her girlish first impressions.

In the years that followed, she had made herself useful—some might say indispensable—to Lady Ramsay, and as that lady's health had failed, Jane had taken over more and more the running of the household. And if her determination to make Richard as comfortable as possible sprang less from duty than from rather warmer sentiments, she had taken care that no one should suspect the state of her heart, for this would mean the end of her comfortable existence. The highest sticklers might suggest that there was something improper about her continued presence at Ramsay Hall two years after the death of her employer; kinder souls, however, would have pointed out that Miss Hawthorne *was*, after all, his lordship's cousin, and if anything of, well, of an *amorous* nature were likely to happen between them, it surely would have taken place years ago under her ladyship's watchful eye, and would have culminated at the altar. Jane sighed. There was no denying the fact that this attitude made her life easier, as it allowed her to continue at the house that had been her home for the last ten years; still, it would have been nice if *someone* had believed her capable of inspiring in Lord Ramsay an unseemly passion.

She had known, of course, that someday Richard would take a bride; after all, no man so conscious of his responsibilities as to propose marriage to a stranger would be so negligent as to ignore his primary obligation to provide for the succession. In the same manner, she had always understood that the new Lady Ramsay would not wish the former chatelaine to continue under her roof. She had supposed that, when the time came, she would retire to the Dower House with the Aunts, although she suspected Aunt Charlotte would not desire any interference with her own running of that establishment any more than Richard's bride would with that of Ramsay Hall. To be sure, Richard's request had postponed the dreaded day of her removal, but at what cost? Surely there could be few things more painful than to tutor the very one whose claim meant the end of hopes so long suppressed that she had believed them dead.

Such melancholy thoughts still haunted her the following morning, as she consulted with Mrs. Meeks, the housekeeper, concerning meals for the coming week and assuring that old retainer that there was no reason to suppose the new Lady Ramsay (really, how *did* the servants contrive to ferret out such events almost before the family knew of them?) would wish to replace her. At last, having dismissed Mrs. Meeks to her domain below stairs, Jane sought refuge in the garden, and it was here, a short time later, that Sir Matthew Pitney found her.

"Exquisite! A rose in its natural setting," declared her longtime suitor, a well-built gentleman of forty who might have been accounted handsome, had it not been for a heaviness about his jowls. In truth, Jane found these unfortunate facial features less objectionable than his even heavier-handed gallantry.

"No rose, Sir Matthew, merely a hawthorn," quipped Jane, offering her hand.

"I will allow no one to contradict me in this, Miss Hawthorne, not even your fair self. I said a rose, and I meant it." So saying, he raised her hand to his lips.

"You are too kind," she protested, gently but firmly withdrawing the hand he showed no signs of releasing. "Tell me, Sir Matthew, what brings you here this fine morning?"

"As if your own self were not enticement enough!" Seeing not pretty confusion but skeptical amusement reflected in her countenance, he abandoned (at least for the nonce) his unsuccessful attempt at flirtation. "Truth to tell, Miss Hawthorne, I have heard a piece of news so astonishing that I came at once for confirmation. Is it true that Lord Ramsay is to take a bride from America?"

"Gossiping with the servants, Sir Matthew? Fie on you!"

He neither confirmed nor denied the charge. "It is

too bad, your nose being put out of joint by an interloper, and an American, at that."

"Nonsense! I have always known that Richard would marry someday."

Apparently she was more distressed than she let on, for somehow Sir Matthew contrived to possess himself of her hand again, and held it clasped between both of his own. As she berated herself for a moment's inattention, he bent over her and addressed her in throbbing accents. "I'm sure I need not tell you that there is *one* place you might occupy secure in the knowledge that you would never be supplanted!"

"No, indeed, you need not tell me at all! And it is too kind of you, Sir Matthew, but quite unnecessary. I am not to be supplanted, as you suggest; in fact, quite the opposite, for my cousin has begged me to stay on and instruct Miss Ramsay in anything she might need to know about the running of a large household."

She was pleased to note that there was no wobble or break in her voice as she said the words—nothing, in fact, that might suggest to her listener that she felt anything but pleasurable anticipation for the task set before her. Even so, she found it more than a little ironic that she, who had more reason than anyone to wish Miss Susannah Ramsay at perdition, should be compelled to act as the girl's most outspoken advocate.

But it appeared that her point had been made, for after making a few unobjectionable inquiries as to when young Miss Ramsay might be expected to arrive, as well as any plans made for her introduction to the neighborhood gentry, Sir Matthew abandoned the subject of Lord Ramsay's approaching nuptials, and turned instead to the topic of flowers.

"I detect Miss Amelia's hand at work amongst your roses," he observed, stooping to smell one. Jane had a sudden mental image of a bumblebee stinging him on the nose, and strove to keep a straight face. His next words helped considerably in this regard. "I wish you will prevail upon her to give me a cutting. I am something of a horticulturist myself, you know, and I have not seen this particular color anywhere else."

"No, for she cultivated it herself. She calls it Ramsay Red, but I should have said it was more purple than red, wouldn't you?"

"By whatever name, it is certainly striking. Still, I have asked repeatedly for a cutting, but without success. Will you not speak to her in my behalf?"

She shook her head. "I fear yours is a hopeless cause, Sir Matthew. As I said, she calls it the Ramsay Red, and you are not a Ramsay, you know."

"No, but I flatter myself the houses of Ramsay and Pitney may be joined very soon."

"Will they? I was not aware of it."

There was a distinct chill in her voice, but if Sir Matthew noticed, he was unfazed by it, wagging his finger at her in what he no doubt considered a playful manner.

"You say that now, Miss Hawthorne, but when you find yourself a pensioner in another woman's domain— well, let us say I shall not give up hope just yet."

"Oh, but I wish you would," she sighed, after he had finally taken his leave. "I *do* wish you would!"

For the next six weeks, she moved about the great house like an automaton, doing by rote those chores in which she had once taken such pleasure, constantly aware that in a matter of weeks, she would surrender the house, as well as its master, to another. For his part, Lord Ramsay continued to go about his usual pursuits, riding about his estate, addressing his tenants' concerns, attending Sunday services with the rest of the family, entertaining and being entertained by the neighborhood gentry. Jane was not sure which would have been worse: seeing him in a glow of anticipation, in dread of his bride's arrival, or in this curious state of normality, just as if nothing had changed, when in fact his life— and hers—would never be the same.

In such a manner spring gave way to summer, and at last the day came when Lord Ramsay called his cousin Peter to his study and offered him a bulging coin purse.

"This should cover the cost of a post-chaise from Portsmouth," he said. "I daresay you will prefer to ride, so you may take Sheba, if you wish. Miss Ramsay will no doubt be exhausted from her long journey, so you may bespeak lodging for yourself, Miss Ramsay, and her maid at the Pelican before you begin the return trip."

Peter took the purse, but not without reluctance. "I cannot help thinking it would be best for you to meet your bride at the dock yourself."

"So you've said, and I daresay you are right. But an important vote will be coming before Parliament two days hence, and I cannot neglect my obligation to the House of Lords. As you depart for Portsmouth, I will be setting out for London."

"Yes, my lord," said Peter, suppressing a sigh.

Richard grinned, undeceived. "Am I to be 'my lord,' then? I see I am in your black books, and no mistake!"

"Not at all," Peter protested with perhaps less than perfect truth. "I cannot but feel sorry for the girl, though, having no acquaintances in England to speak of."

"Which only proves that you are the best one to

meet her, for if I were to do so, my mind would be on my empty seat in the Lords—hardly the measure of devotion a young woman might look for in her affianced husband." Seeing his young cousin was not entirely convinced, he added cajolingly, "Come, Peter! Oblige me in this, and I promise that when I return, I will be as attentive toward Miss Ramsay as you might wish."

Peter could not like it, but the end was never in doubt. Having been educated at Lord Ramsay's expense and then engaged as his steward immediately upon leaving university, Peter was in no position to deny his aristocratic cousin any request; nor, in the usual course of events, had he any desire to do so, for besides being his distant relation, his lordship was a fair man and a generous employer. Still, Peter could not entirely applaud Lord Ramsay's hasty betrothal, no matter how admirable the devotion to duty that inspired it. He supposed, with a wry twist of his lips, that it was perhaps a good thing his opinion had never been asked. He was not quite certain whom he pitied the most: the gentleman who had offered marriage out of obligation, or the young lady who had accepted out of expedience.

And so it was that at dawn the following morning, he strapped his valise to the chestnut mare's broad back, swung himself up into the saddle, and set out for

Portsmouth. By early afternoon, he began his descent of Portsdown Hill, from which vantage point he could see the network of forts surrounding the city—a relic of the days not so long past, when England was at war with Napoleon, and Nelson had led forth the aptly named *Victory* from this very port to immortality at Trafalgar. Upon entering the city, he located the waterfront inn called the Pelican, surrendered Sheba to the ostler, and engaged two rooms before setting out on foot for the bustling wharf—and not a moment too soon, for the *Concordia* rode at anchor, and her passengers were even now being transferred from ship to shore by means of a bosun's chair.

Peter scanned the wharf where a dozen travellers now moved about on wobbly legs, wondering if Miss Susannah Ramsay had already been brought ashore, and how he was to identify her. Male passengers greatly outnumbered female, so it should not be difficult, given the limited selection. There stood a middle-aged woman who appeared to be the wife of a prosperous merchant—too old; a younger woman with a child clinging to her skirts and an infant in her arms— obviously not. A female accompanied by a maidservant and dressed in the fashionable pelisse and bonnet of a young lady of quality appeared to be a promising candidate, until she was abruptly seized by a young lieutenant and enveloped in a very public embrace, a scandalous display to which she apparently had not the least objection. Peter could not help smiling a little, wondering how long the Royal Navy had kept the young officer from his bride.

The only other female he could see was a soberly dressed woman of about forty standing a little apart with her husband, a scholarly-looking man engaged in cleaning the sea spray from his spectacles by polishing them on his sleeve. This might be Miss Ramsay's missionary escort, but if that were the case, where was their charge? As if in answer to his question, the woman stepped aside, giving Peter a clear view of the oddest looking girl he had ever seen.

To call her clothing out of fashion would be a misnomer, as it would imply that such garments had ever been *in* fashion. Dark skirts of some coarse cloth were cut much fuller than fashion dictated, and were liberally sprayed with seawater. Peter could form no opinion as to the rest of her dress, for it was covered by what was apparently a man's jacket made of what looked like buckskin, heavily fringed and much too large for its wearer. Her bonnet, black and plain as a Quaker's, hung down her back by its strings, revealing unruly curls of a hue more red than brown. Any less suitable bride for his meticulous cousin would have been hard to imagine.

"Oh, Richard," murmured Peter, "what have you done?"

3

"O mercy!" to myself I cried.
WILLIAM WORDSWORTH,
Strange Fits of Passion Have I Known

With a sinking feeling in the pit of his stomach, Peter approached the soberly clad couple.

"Mr. and Mrs. Latham?"

The man put his spectacles back on and regarded Peter through the round lenses. "Yes?"

"I'm Peter Ramsay," he said, offering his hand. "I've come for Miss Susannah Ramsay."

"Why, look here, Susannah," said Mrs. Latham, turning to address her charge. "Here's Mr. Ramsay, come to fetch you."

Miss Ramsay had been gaping at the bustling waterfront with wide blue eyes and mouth open in an "O" of amazement, but upon hearing Peter's name, she turned to regard her kinsman and sank into a deep curtsy.

"My lord," she said breathlessly.

"What—who, me?" stammered Peter, hastily demurring. "No, I'm not—that is, my cousin Richard is Lord Ramsay. I am your cousin Peter, and his lordship's steward."

"Oh," said Miss Ramsay, somewhat crestfallen.

"Richard was obliged to go to London to take his seat in Parliament, so he sent me in his place. He sends his regrets, and hopes you will forgive his lack of hospitality."

This was not entirely true, perhaps, but Peter judged it politic, given the American girl's obvious disappointment, to stretch a point.

"Well, Susannah," said Mrs. Latham, offering a gloved hand to her young protégée, "I suppose this is goodbye. Thank you for bearing me company on the journey, my dear."

Susannah ignored the hand, and threw her arms around the woman instead. "The obligation is all mine, ma'am. Oh, how I shall miss you!"

Mrs. Latham patted her consolingly on the back. "Nonsense! You will be much too busy learning to be a great lady to spare a thought for an old sobersides like me. You must be sure to write, once you are settled, and let me know how you go on."

Susannah promised fervently to do so, and after

tearful goodbyes (at least on Susannah's part), the missionary couple departed. As they reached the end of the quay, Mrs. Latham glanced almost furtively back at her erstwhile charge, then took her husband's arm and hurried him across the road. Peter, puzzling over the woman's curious behavior, shook his head as if to clear it, then hefted Susannah's portmanteau and set it on his shoulder.

"Well, Miss Ramsay—look here, may I call you Cousin Susannah?—if you will summon your maid, I will escort you to the Pelican Inn, where I've bespoke lodgings for the night."

"My maid? Oh, but I haven't one."

"No—no maid?" stammered Peter.

Miss Ramsay shrugged. "I'm used to fending for myself. Take my clothes, for example: I'm not wearing anything that I can't put on without help."

Peter, surveying her curious travelling costume at close range, could not doubt that an unassisted female might easily don such garments; the only question, to his mind, was why any female would want to. The greater dilemma, however, was the fact that his cousin's future bride would be putting up at a public inn with no chaperone—no companion at all, in fact, but her twenty-three year old male cousin. As no hint of impropriety must be allowed to attach itself to the future Lady Ramsay, he resolved to speak to the innkeeper and ask if that worthy individual might spare a chambermaid to wait upon Miss Ramsay—for a consideration, of course, as compensation for leaving the establishment short-handed.

"Very well, then, Miss—er, Cousin Susannah. If you will allow me, I shall escort you to the Pelican. You will no doubt wish to rest after your long journey, and when you are ready, I will have a tray sent up to your room, so you may eat in privacy."

"Oh, must I?" asked Susannah, her expressive countenance registering dismay. "I have been shut up in a tiny cabin for weeks, and have had quite enough of my own company. There is so much I want to ask—so much that could not be told in a letter. May we not have our dinner together, downstairs?"

Peter could not but see the justice of this request, and so, after seeing his American cousin installed in the Pelican's best guest chamber with the innkeeper's daughter to wait upon her, he requested a private parlor where they might, at least, be safe from prying eyes. Alas, someone else had been before him: the private parlor had already been reserved. And so, with a sinking heart, he claimed a table in the back corner, one with high-backed wooden benches which might shield Miss Ramsay, at least partially, from the stares of the curious. Still, this solution left much to be desired, as the same discreet location that he hoped would protect her privacy also hinted at clandestine purpose.

With a sigh of resignation, he settled himself on the side of the table which gave a clear view of the door, drew a book out of the pocket of his coat, and settled in to read until Susannah joined him for dinner.

He had not long to wait. Scarcely half an hour had passed before she sailed into the inn's public room. He was relieved to note that she had shed her odd buckskin coat and changed her wet garments for dry ones, but he could not honestly say that her new ensemble was much of an improvement. Full dark skirts swirled about her stout leather half-boots, exposing a glimpse of thick black stockings. Tucked into the skirt at the waist was a loose blouse of coarse cotton, none too white. She had apparently made an attempt to tame her hair, scraping it up into a tight bun from which curling tendrils were already beginning to escape.

"I could not rest," she declared, seating herself on the bench facing him. "There is too much to see, too much to learn."

Any hope that she might sit demurely with her back to the room faded as she turned to survey her surroundings, then began waving wildly at two men, sailors by the look of them, who had just entered the room in search of liquid refreshment.

"Er, someone you know, Cousin?" Peter inquired, seeing the two men heading in their direction.

"Cousin Peter, this is Tom Crawford and Billy Watkins. Tom is bosun's mate aboard the *Concordia*, and Billy is—oh, Billy, I'm so sorry! I can't remember your title."

"Lord love you, miss, I'm just a common seaman," said Billy, grinning at her in a way Peter could only describe as familiar.

"Tom and Billy were very kind to me during the long voyage, showing me all about the ship: the sails, and the rigging, and the—the poop deck, which sounds very unladylike to say, although they assure me it is no such thing—"

She colored nevertheless, which made the sailors laugh. Peter was relieved to see that she could blush.

"Tom, Billy," she continued, "this is my cousin, Peter Ramsay."

"Mr. Ramsay, sir." The two men tugged at their forelocks.

Peter thanked the two men for their kindness to Miss Ramsay, and insisted upon demonstrating his gratitude by paying for their drinks—a seemingly generous gesture which made Susannah beam approvingly, but which the two sailors, Britons themselves, recognized as payment for services rendered, and therefore a signal that their familiarity with Miss Ramsay was at an end.

Once the men had taken their leave, Peter bent what he hoped was a stern gaze upon his wayward cousin. "I thought you said you spent all your time in your cabin."

"Not *all* my time," she admitted, unrepentant. "But poor Mrs. Latham suffered from seasickness, and I could not stay shut up forever, just because she was too ill to accompany me on deck. It was all perfectly innocent. Tom and Billy and the other sailors were very kind, and so helpful."

"I'll just bet they were," Peter muttered.

"What did you say?"

He shook his head. "Never mind. I suppose you did not know any better. But now that you are in England, Cousin Susannah, such free and easy behavior will not do."

"I knew it would be different, of course," she confessed, somewhat daunted. "Will you tell me about him—this cousin I am supposed to marry? I could not determine much from his letters, you know. They were so formal and stiff."

He gave a little laugh. "Then they gave you a very good insight into his character, for he *is* formal and stiff." Seeing her dismayed expression, he added hastily, "Oh, he is a very good man, and will not be neglectful of his wife's comfort. He will do nothing to make you unhappy. But he is very careful of his obligation to his title, and to his family."

Susannah wrinkled her nose. "He sounds like a very dull stick!"

"He is not, I assure you. He may seem that way at first, I grant you, but he is not without a sense of humour."

"What does he look like? Is he handsome?"

"He is thirty-one years old—I daresay he told you that in his letter—while as for his being handsome, well, I fear I am the wrong person to answer that, but I believe he is generally accounted to be very well-looking."

"Does he look anything like you?" Apparently realizing too late that this question, following as it did Peter's assessment of Lord Ramsay as well-looking, might suggest a flattering appraisal of his own appearance, she hastily amended, "Is there a family resemblance, I mean?"

"If so, it is a very tenuous one. Richard is taller than I by half a head, and while we both have the dark hair and eyes that may be seen in any number of family portraits, he wears them rather better than I. In fact, he looks like an aristocrat, while I look like—" He shrugged. "—a poor relation."

Her eyes widened. "Is that what you are?"

"Oh, I am not poor anymore, thanks to Richard. He paid for my education, you know, and gave me the position of steward when I left university. He has been very good to me, and I am grateful to him. But you—I understand you are a considerable heiress, Cousin Susannah. What made you decide to travel halfway 'round the world to marry a man you have never met?"

"It is true that I am an heiress, Cousin Peter, but I am also a minor, with no relations—at least, no American relations—to assume guardianship. I had to marry someone."

"But—forgive me, but with your holdings, I should have thought you would not lack for suitors."

She gave a bitter laugh. "Oh no, I did not lack for suitors! But all of them were far more interested in my holdings, as you put it, than in myself. When I got Lord Ramsay's letter, I thought that an English lord, whatever his faults, could at least have no interest in my inheritance."

"A title does not always mean wealth, Cousin Susannah, but in Richard's case, your instincts were correct. He is quite solvent—wealthy, even—so you may acquit him of being a fortune-hunter."

Susannah pressed a hand to her bosom and let out a sigh of relief. "Thank heaven for that! Oh, I *knew* I did right to come here!"

"Tell me about your home in America," he urged. "Virginia, is it?"

She shook her head. "It is true that I have a town house in Richmond, but I have not lived there since I was two. Papa and I have always lived on the Kentucky property."

Peter, being accustomed to English gentlemen who owned town houses in London in addition to their country estates, saw nothing to wonder at in this arrangement. "Is it a large estate?"

"Eight hundred acres, but only about half of it is under cultivation at present. Papa had hoped to clear more this year, and to build a house, a big one with Ionic columns along the front and a wide veranda, but—" She broke off, shrugging.

Recalling the death that had put paid to her father's plans, Peter thought it best to divert her mind from the recent tragedy. "Under cultivation, you say? With what crops?"

"Corn, mostly—we distill our own bourbon, you know—and some tobacco. And we raise horses," she added proudly.

"Do you like to ride, then?"

"Oh, yes! Papa put me in the saddle when I was only three," she said, smiling.

"You will find plenty of opportunity at Ramsay Hall, then, for my cousin's stables are extensive."

Throughout dinner, they discussed such innocuous subjects as might introduce Susannah to her new situation without overwhelming her, while Peter discovered what he might about the American holdings that would pass to Lord Ramsay upon his marriage. At last she broke off in mid-sentence, yawning widely.

"But I must not keep you up talking when you have had such a full day," Peter said, starting guiltily as he realized the lateness of the hour and the emptiness of the public room. "You will have been wanting your bed any time this last half-hour and more."

"Oh no, truly I have not," Susannah objected, but another yawn gave the lie to her words.

Peter had to laugh at this blatant falsehood. "Still, you should get what sleep you can, for we will set out early in the morning for Ramsay Hall. It will not do, you know, for you to be asleep on your feet when you make your curtsy to your affianced husband."

"No, I suppose not. It is just that you are so easy to talk to," she added naïvely. "Quite as easy as my friends on the *Concordia*. I only hope Lord Ramsay will turn out to be half so agreeable!"

"Thank you, Cousin Susannah," Peter said modestly, fighting back a grin at the idea that Lord Ramsay should aspire to be as affable as a pair of tars. "If you will allow me, I will accompany you as far as your door."

Susannah was nothing loth, and so after escorting her up the stairs and down the corridor as far as her door, Peter bade her a good night and retraced his steps to his own room. Once inside, he removed his coat and laid it across the back of the room's single straight chair, thinking of his cousin's peculiar bride. Seen at close range (and provided one ignored everything from the neck down), she was not a bad-looking girl. Her blue eyes held intelligence and an openness which was pleasing. To be sure, her nose boasted more than a scattering of freckles—a souvenir from her time on deck, he had no doubt—but his cousin Jane should know what to do about them. The hair was unfortunate, but perhaps Jane would know what to do about that, too. It appeared that Richard might not have made a bad bargain after all, provided he could dissuade his bride from fraternizing with sailors.

With this comforting thought, he finished his nocturnal preparations, snuffed the candle, and climbed into bed, and soon slept the sleep of the just.

4

Journeys end in lovers meeting.
WILLIAM SHAKESPEARE, *Twelfth Night*

*P*eter arose early the next morning to prepare for the journey home, and was appalled to discover Susannah awake before him, sitting quite alone in the public room and addressing herself to a hearty breakfast.

"This is not bacon," she informed him, eyeing the rasher on her plate with disfavour. "This is ham."

"Call it whatever you like in America, but when you ask for bacon here, this is what you're going to get." Realizing he had sounded harsher than he'd intended, he added, "You need not eat it if you dislike it. Shall I ask the cook to bring you something else?"

She shook her head. "No, no, that's all right. I don't dislike it, precisely; it's just that I was expecting something different."

"And it takes a moment to adjust your

expectations," he said, nodding in understanding. He suspected the same experience was awaiting his cousin Richard, only it would not be breakfast meats at issue. "I'm sorry I was not in time to bespeak breakfast for you, but I'm glad you were not obliged to wait on me. May I join you?"

"Oh, please do!"

He sat, and had not long to wait before his own breakfast was brought out.

"You drink *beer* for breakfast?" exclaimed Susannah, wrinkling her nose in distaste as a tankard of the inn's home-brewed was set at his elbow.

He laughed at her obvious disgust. "Ale, yes. Most Englishmen do, including Richard, so I'm afraid you shall have to get used to it."

"Never!" declared Susannah, lifting her coffee cup with a flourish. "Give me coffee any day."

"Lord, yes! No lady would drink ale for breakfast—well, except for Aunt Charlotte, and she is old enough, she says, to do as she pleases."

She laughed delightedly. "I may not approve of ale for breakfast, but I like your Aunt Charlotte already. Does she live at Ramsay Hall, as well?"

"No, she lives in the Dower House with her sister, Aunt Amelia," he told her in between bites of buttered eggs and the meat that was indeed bacon, in spite of her low opinion of it. "And I should explain that they are not my aunts, but rather some distant cousin. They are Richard's aunts, but they will take it very ill if you call them anything but Aunt Charlotte and Aunt Amelia. We all do."

" 'All'?" echoed Susannah in some alarm. "How many people are we talking about?"

"Not that many, really," he hastened to assure her. "At Ramsay Hall, there is only Richard, and myself, and—and Cousin Jane."

"Cousin Jane?"

He was not quite certain why he should be reluctant to bring Cousin Jane into the conversation; certainly there was nothing in the least inappropriate about her presence in the house. He supposed he was fearful that Susannah might take exception to another female holding the reins of the household and, perhaps, being unwilling to surrender them to the new mistress.

"She is a Ramsay on the distaff side, her mother having married a man by the name of Hawthorne," he explained. "She served as companion to the previous Lady Ramsay—Richard's mother—and after her ladyship's death, she stayed on to take over the running of the house."

Susannah nodded in understanding. "A housekeeper, of sorts."

"No, no, for Mrs. Meeks is that. Jane's status is somewhat ambiguous. In some ways Jane acts as mistress of the house, although she has no real claim to that title and, to do her justice, has never tried to put herself forward in that regard." Seeing the puzzled frown that creased Susannah's brow, he added hastily, "You need not fear that she will try to usurp your own authority, or undermine your relationship with Richard, or anything of that nature, for she is the kindest creature imaginable."

Seeing Susannah push her plate away (empty, in spite of her objections to the bacon), Peter put down his fork, picked up his tankard, and drained the last of his ale. "You are wise to make a substantial meal of it, Cousin Susannah, for we have a lot of ground to cover before stopping for luncheon. If you will excuse me, I must go to the post office to arrange for the hiring of a chaise."

After recommending that she enlist the innkeeper's daughter to pack her bags, he took his leave of her. The post chaise arrived within the hour, and after seeing her bag stowed on its boot, Peter instructed the ostler to saddle Sheba for the journey, then turned to hand Miss Ramsay into the hired conveyance.

"Aren't you coming with me?" she asked with a note of panic in her voice.

"Of course I am. But I shall be riding on horseback."

"Not—not in the carriage with me?"

"Certainly not," said Peter, slightly shocked at the very suggestion. "It would be most improper for us to be shut up in a closed carriage, unchaperoned, for a lengthy journey."

"But if we are shut up inside a closed carriage, how would anyone know?" she asked with unassailable logic.

"*I* would know," he insisted. "What's more, Richard would know, and he would be very displeased with me if I should do anything that might leave his bride open to censure."

"Are you so afraid of him then?" asked Susannah, wide-eyed.

"Afraid of Richard? Heavens, no! But recall that he is my employer as well as my cousin, so I must consider myself bound by his wishes. And in this case, he would be quite right."

She sighed. "I'm afraid I'm in for a very dull ride, with no one to talk to."

"Do you like to read?" Peter asked, recalling the book tucked away in his valise. "I can lend you the second volume of *Waverley*, if you don't mind starting in the middle."

"Not at all," Susannah assured him. "Beggars can't be choosers, you know."

"And once we reach Ramsay Hall, you can always get the first volume from Richard's library, if you wish."

"He has a *library*? A whole library, all to himself?"

Peter nodded, smiling. "A very extensive one."

"I think perhaps I like Richard better already," she declared. "No one can be a dull stick who has his own library."

"I can see you have never met Sir Matthew Pitney," Peter said with a grin.

"Who is he?"

"Our nearest neighbor, and a very dull stick indeed. But he does have a library."

"I think you must be teasing me!"

"Not at all. Only wait until you meet him. Oh, here is the ostler with Sheba. Give me a minute to fetch *Waverley* from my valise, and we will be on our way."

He did more than that. He went back inside the inn, and eventually persuaded the innkeeper to allow his daughter to accompany Miss Ramsay in the post-chaise. He was, of course, obliged to pay for young Betsy's return trip by stagecoach, to say nothing of compensating her father for the temporary loss of her labour, but he had the satisfaction of knowing that the proprieties would be observed. And so the trio set out from the Pelican's stable yard. They broke their journey at Winchester for a light nuncheon, during which Peter fully expected to be pelted with questions as to whether Edward Waverley would end up marrying the tempestuous Flora MacIvor or the more serene Rose Bradwardine.

Here, however, he was mistaken, for once they had been shown into a private parlor and plied with cold chicken, bread, and cheese, Susannah confessed somewhat guiltily that she had not progressed beyond the first twenty pages.

"For I am reading aloud so that Betsy might enjoy the story, too, and my attempts at voicing the Scottish characters were enough to send us both into whoops. So I have decided poor Edward Waverley must wait until I can get the first volume from Lord Ramsay's library and read it in silence. In the meantime, Betsy has been pointing out landmarks to me, and telling me all about life in England."

"I see," Peter said, nodding. Privately, he thought the life of a Portsmouth innkeeper's daughter would bear little resemblance to the future that awaited Susannah as Lady Ramsay, but as the innkeeper's daughter sat beside her at the table (where his American cousin had insisted on placing the girl), he was forced to keep this observation to himself.

"Only fancy, Cousin Peter! Betsy has an elder brother in the navy, who fought against us."

" 'Us'?"

"Well, me, anyway. Americans, I mean. It seems very strange to think of us as enemies, does it not?"

"I am sure no one could think of you as an enemy, Cousin Susannah," Peter said, and was surprised to discover that he meant it. However odd her appearance, and still more so her manners, she was a rather taking little thing. He only hoped his cousin Richard would agree. "Still, it is probably best to avoid topics on which you are bound to find yourself at odds with your new acquaintances."

"Well, we didn't talk about the war much, because neither of us knew much about it," Susannah admitted, dismissing the late hostilities with a shrug of her shoulders. "Mostly we have been talking about our families. Betsy has *seven* siblings, and two of them are twins!"

She turned to the innkeeper's daughter for confirmation, and Betsy bobbed her head in agreement. Peter suppressed a sigh, acknowledging that someone (and he very much feared that he knew upon whom the task would most likely fall) would have to speak to his cousin regarding her familiarity with persons beneath her station. It was with a certain reluctance, therefore, that he handed both young women back into the post chaise, where they would, he had no doubt, resume their quite inappropriate friendship.

The rest of the journey passed without incident, and shortly after five o'clock in the evening they had turned into the sweeping drive that led to Ramsay Hall. Peter regretted that he could not hear her observations upon first catching sight of her future home, but her nose pressed to the glass of the carriage window, her wide eyes, and her open mouth told their own tale.

As the post-chaise drew to a stop before the house, the great front doors burst open, and an army of footmen emerged; clearly, someone had been keeping watch for their arrival. Peter swung himself down from the saddle and tossed Sheba's reins to the groom hurrying up from the stables, while one of the footmen began to unfasten the straps holding his valise in place. The driver had dismounted as well, and as he flung open the door of the carriage and let down the step, Peter strode forward to hand both young women down.

Susannah immediately folded the innkeeper's daughter in a fond embrace. "Thank you so much for accompanying me, Betsy. Please give my regards to your parents, and tell your little brother that I hope his toothache is better soon."

Peter interrupted what promised to be a very protracted farewell by pressing a crown piece into Betsy's hand and directing her to the servants' entrance, where the housekeeper would give her refreshments in the kitchen and a bed for the night before her return journey to Portsmouth in the morning. Having dispatched the innkeeper's daughter to her proper sphere, he turned back to his charge and offered his arm with great ceremony.

"Welcome to Ramsay Hall, Cousin Susannah."

She pressed one trembling hand to the bosom of that regrettable buckskin coat, took a deep breath, and laid her other hand lightly on his sleeve. Another footman flung open the door as they climbed the shallow steps to the portico, and Peter handed her over the threshold.

Yet another footman took Peter's hat and gloves, and would have relieved Susannah of her odd buckskin garment, but she had no attention to spare for him, engaged as she was in gaping about the entrance hall. Peter suppressed a smile, recalling his own similar first impressions of the marble-tiled floors, intricately plastered ceilings, and, most of all, the broad curving staircase with its beveled banister of polished oak.

"Oh!" she breathed. "Do you ever slide down it?"

Whatever he had expected her to say, it was not

that. "Er, slide down it?"

"The banister, I mean."

His eyebrows shot up in alarm. "Good heavens, no! Nothing could be more improper."

"Why?"

There were so many reasons, he hardly knew where to start. "I am an employee in this house—" he began.

She bravely lifted a chin that showed only the slightest tendency to wobble. "If I am to be mistress here, I should like to slide down it at least once a day."

"Er, you must of course do as you think best, Cousin Susannah, but perhaps it would be wise of you to meet the members of the household before you begin setting it on its ear."

Much distressed, Susannah clapped a hand to her mouth. "I'm sorry! I did not mean—" She broke off, seeing the twinkle lurking in his brown eyes. "I think you are teasing me, Cousin Peter!"

He bowed in acknowledgement. "I am, indeed. And in the interest of full disclosure, I must admit that I have long wondered what it must be like to slide down the banister."

"Very well, then, when I am mistress here, you can join me, and we will slide down it together."

"Perhaps we can form a club," he suggested,

making her giggle. "But in the meantime, I believe the ladies of the household are waiting to make your acquaintance. Shall we?"

He nodded toward the door to the drawing room, beyond which a flurry of feminine voices had fallen silent in anticipation of their appearance. Susannah followed him across the hall and, at a sweeping gesture from Peter, preceded him into the room.

This room was no less intimidating that the entrance hall, but its rather daunting effect had less to do with the thick Aubusson carpet, graceful Hepple-white furnishings, and elegant Adam fireplace than with the room's inhabitants. Three ladies sat within, two of them elderly, and the third much younger, all eyeing the newcomer with varying degrees of curiosity and outright disbelief. The two elderly ladies, each wearing a frilled white cap over iron-grey curls, Susannah had no difficulty in identifying as the aunts: Charlotte, he'd said, and the second—Emily, was it? No, something else—Amelia. Yes, that was it, although she was not sure which was Charlotte and which was Amelia.

That would make the third lady—her eyes widened at the discovery that Cousin Jane was not at all the middle-aged spinster she'd imagined, but a very attractive woman who looked to be still in her twenties. Susannah was still trying to assimilate this discovery when the lady rose to her feet, revealing the full glory of a high-waisted, narrow-skirted gown of some peach-colored fabric which a more knowledgeable young lady would have recognized at once as silk, but which even to Susannah's untrained eye whispered of wealth, breeding, and quiet elegance. Susannah unconsciously fingered the folds of her buckskin coat, realizing for the first time how she must appear to these refined aristocrats. Peter must surely have noticed, but he had been too well-mannered to let on; she hardly knew whether to feel grateful or mortified.

"Miss Ramsay," he said, taking her elbow and leading her forward into the center of the room, "allow me to present Aunt Charlotte Ramsay, Aunt Amelia Ramsay, and Miss Jane Hawthorne. Aunt Charlotte, Aunt Amelia, Cousin Jane—Miss Susannah Ramsay."

Stiff curtsies were exchanged all around, during which Susannah felt a feather-light touch against her left eyebrow, and realized her unruly hair had once again slipped its moorings. Noting her Cousin Jane's elegantly coiffed ash blonde tresses, she thrust her lower lip sharply to the left and let out several huffing breaths, as if she could somehow blow the offending curl back into place—a strategy that had not worked once in eighteen years, but one to which she still sought frequent and hopeful recourse.

Cousin Jane took Susannah's hands in welcome. "Cousin Susannah—I may call you cousin, may I not?—you must be famished from the journey. We will dine at eight, but do allow me to offer you something in the meantime. Cakes, perhaps, and tea?"

"Yes, thank you," Susannah agreed meekly.

It was as if the room itself let out its breath. Aunt Amelia (who proved to be the one in mulberry satin, while her sister, Aunt Charlotte, wore purple) moved forward to press a kiss to her cheek, exclaiming, "Let me look at you, my dear. Yes, I believe you have great-grandfather Edward Ramsay's nose. I wonder I didn't recognize it at once."

"Most likely because it is covered in freckles," observed Aunt Charlotte, but this criticism was leavened with a hint of a smile. "I hope your journey was not too tedious, and that our Peter took care of you?"

"Oh, yes! And not only Peter, but everyone has been most kind," Susannah agreed readily, although some instinct warned her not to mention Betsy, and still less the crew of the *Concordia*.

The promised refreshments arrived in short order, and Susannah set to with a will; as Peter had already had cause to discover, she was possessed of a healthy appetite which several hours on the road had done nothing to diminish. Conversation was of necessity scant, as the Ramsay ladies had the courtesy not to ply their young relation with questions while she was eating—or perhaps they had no very great confidence that she would not attempt to answer any such questions with her mouth full.

In any case, they had not succeeded in learning much about her when the butler appeared, looking uncharacteristically flustered and casting furtive glances at the new arrival. "Miss Hawthorne," he said, addressing the *de facto* mistress of the house in an undervoice, "I felt I should warn you—inform you, that is—that his lordship—it is sooner than expected, I know, but—well, miss, the truth of the matter is that Master Richard is here!"

"What, already?" asked Jane, ignoring the old retainer's use of Lord Ramsay's childhood designation. "I had not thought to see him until tomorrow, at the earliest."

"Yes, miss. But he is here, sure as I live. He has gone upstairs to freshen up after the journey, but—"

His gaze darted once more to Susannah, and Jane had no difficulty in interpreting the meaning of that look. Indeed, her own thoughts were running along very similar lines. She had not known quite what to expect out of their American cousin, but given the tone of Mrs.

Latham's letter, she (unlike Peter) had been glad to know that Richard would not be present to witness the arrival of his bride, as she had expected to need a little time to make Miss Ramsay presentable to her future husband. She had thought to begin by taking her to a dressmaker; now, it appeared she would not even have time to drag a brush through the girl's hair.

"Thank you, Wilson, but I am sure we shall contrive," she said with a confidence she was far from feeling. "Pray instruct Antoine to move dinner forward as much as possible, for I am sure his lordship must be quite famished."

"Yes, miss." The butler bowed and, with one last dubious glance at his future mistress, betook himself from the room.

"Here is good news," she declared to Susannah, as if stating a falsehood with sufficient confidence might make it so. "Cousin Richard has returned early from London. He has gone upstairs at present, but you may meet him very shortly."

This cheerful prophecy was sufficient to make Susannah choke on the seed cake she was eating, forcing Peter to pound her on the back. Scarcely had she gained control of herself when the door opened, and she had her first glimpse of the man whom she had travelled halfway 'round the world to marry.

He was quite tall, as Peter had said, with hair as sleek and dark as a raven's wing. His eyes, too, were dark, just as Peter's were, but his jaw was sharper and his chin rather stronger. Where the younger man's expression was open and friendly, the head of the family appeared distant, perhaps even bored. A disinterested observer would have accounted Lord Ramsay the handsomer of the two men, but Susannah was far from disinterested, and she determined at once to like Peter better than his noble cousin.

"Why, Richard, what a pleasant surprise," Jane said, rising to greet him. "We had not thought to see you until tomorrow."

"As you can see, I yielded to Peter's entreaties and hurried home immediately after the vote was taken in the Lords. But where, pray, is my affianced bride?" His dismissive gaze took in the young woman seated on the sofa, and returned to his cousin Jane. "I see her abigail has made herself quite at home, but if Miss Ramsay thinks to entertain the servants to tea on a regular basis, I must be sure to inform her that such democratic notions will not—"

"Richard," Jane interrupted, fixing him with a speaking look, "allow me to present Miss Susannah Ramsay. Miss Ramsay, our mutual cousin Richard, Lord Ramsay."

Susannah rose from the sofa with surprising grace, her heightened color the only hint that she was aware of the insult.

"My lord." She placed her hand in his own belatedly proffered one, and sank to the floor in a curtsy so low that the fringed hem of her buckskin coat brushed the carpet.

"Miss Ramsay," Richard said stiffly, bowing deeply over her hand. Jane had no difficulty in recognizing his excessive formality as an attempt to cover his embarrassment at his own glaring *faux pas*, but Susannah had not the advantage of long acquaintance with his lordship. To her, this overdone courtesy smacked of arrogance, with perhaps a little mockery thrown in for good measure.

Perhaps, Jane thought later, all might have been well if she had not instructed Antoine to move dinner forward. Perhaps if they had dined at eight, as originally planned, there would have been time for Richard to apologize for his error, and the whole matter might have been laughed off. But no, Richard had scarcely released his bride's hand when Wilson returned to announce dinner.

"If you will do me the honour, Miss Ramsay?" Lord Ramsay asked, offering his arm.

"With pleasure, my lord." With a sparkling eye and

a disdainful sniff, Susannah placed her hand on his.

Behind their backs, Jane and Peter exchanged looks of mutual dismay, then followed the mismatched pair into the dining room.

5

Mother, may I go out to swim?
Yes, my darling daughter:
Hang your clothes on a hickory limb
And don't go near the water.
ANONYMOUS, *Rhyme*

"My poor Jane! Can you ever forgive me?" Lord Ramsay collapsed onto the sofa beside his cousin and raked long, slender fingers through his dark hair. The interminable dinner had finally come to an end, the aunts departed for the Dower House, and Peter and Susannah retired to their respective bedchambers, each professing exhaustion from their journey. His lordship had not retreated to his library, as was his usual habit after dinner, but instead had sought out his cousin Jane, drawn to her serene composure as steel to a magnet.

"That depends," she said, inserting the needle into her embroidery and pulling it through. "What have you done that I am expected to forgive?"

"Need you ask? I have set you an impossible task, for which I apologize with all my heart. A baroness in buckskin!" he said bitterly, shaking his head in appalled disbelief.

She gave him a reproachful look. "I think she deserves your apology far more than I. Really, Richard, how could you be so maladroit as to take her for a servant girl? And she has your great-great-grandfather's nose, too!" she added, with a lurking twinkle in her fine grey eyes.

"Has she? I confess, I did not notice. I was too taken aback by the clothes, and the hair, and the freckles, and the—"

"Clothes can be changed, hair can be cut, and freckles can be faded with crushed strawberries. As for the responsibilities of running a noble household, bear in mind that Miss Ramsay has had charge of her father's house from a young age. In fact, she may find instructing servants to be rather less demanding than being obliged to do everything for herself. So you see, it is not so impossible a task, after all. But I do think you must beg her pardon."

"Oh, unquestionably! I only hope she will not snap my nose off. I wonder she did not do so tonight, for she certainly had murder in her eye."

Jane acknowledged the truth of this with a laugh.

"Well, and can you blame her?"

"After crossing the ocean only to be insulted by her betrothed?" He grimaced at the memory. "No jury in the land would convict her."

Jane knotted the thread and snipped it off with a tiny pair of scissors, then set her needlework aside. "It was not, perhaps, your finest moment, but when one considers that you had only just returned from London yourself—"

He held up a hand to forestall her. "Pray do not make excuses for me! Believe me, I am fully aware of my own gaucherie."

"Very well, then, I will only predict that, after she has had a good night's rest, you may find her inclined to laugh the whole thing off." Seeing he was not convinced, she added, "What is the matter, Richard? Do you want to cry off?"

He recoiled as if she had struck him. "Good God, is that what you think of me—that I could ask a gently born female to travel halfway 'round the world to marry me, only to jilt her practically at the altar?"

"No, but I do think you are generous to a fault when it comes to putting the needs of others ahead of your own. Surely you have a right to expect happiness in your marriage, and if you cannot find it with Miss Ramsay, then she is unlikely to be happy with you, either."

He dashed a weary hand over his eyes. "My dear Jane, how can I know whether we could be happy together or not, when I never laid eyes on her until this evening? Clearly, she and I must get to know each other rather better before the ceremony, but in the meantime—" He heaved a sigh. "In the meantime, I shall depend upon my clever Cousin Jane to work her particular magic on the girl."

He lifted her hand to his lips in a gesture that held all the exaggerated gallantry of his bow to his bride, and yet where that earlier performance had been stiffly formal, his obeisance to his cousin Jane held a great deal of charm. After he had said goodnight and left her in sole possession of the drawing room, Jane sighed and pressed her hand to her cheek. If he would show this side of himself to his chosen bride, she felt certain Miss Susannah Ramsay would tumble head over ears.

Granted, at first glance it would be difficult to imagine a less likely bride for Lord Ramsay, who certainly knew what was due his position and his name. And yet, where he had seen only a female with unruly ginger hair and odd, poorly fitted clothing made of buckskin and homespun, Jane's keener eye (sizing up a rival in spite of her best efforts not to view her cousin Susannah in such a light) had discerned wide, inquisitive blue eyes in a piquant heart-shaped face and, beneath the coarse garments, the promise of a trim, pleasingly rounded figure.

No, if she were honest with herself, she did not fear her failure to transform Miss Ramsay to Richard's liking; in fact, she feared she would succeed only too well for her own peace of mind.

Such were her unpleasant thoughts as she climbed the stairs to her own bedchamber, to fall at last into a troubled sleep. She awakened at dawn to the feel of someone shaking her by the shoulder, and opened her eyes to find the second chambermaid, Liza, standing over her, the candle in the girl's hand casting weird shadows over her face.

"Beggin' your pardon," she said in hushed tones, "but it's that Miss Ramsay. She's up and done a bunk."

Jane sat up abruptly, all traces of sleep fled. "Miss Ramsay is gone?"

"Aye, miss. She woke up when I came in to light the fire. I was that quiet, mind, trying not to disturb her, but Miss Ramsay said she's used to getting up early, which I thought was kind of her to say so, whether it was true or not. So I asked her if she was ready for her bath, and she said she was, so I went down to the kitchen to heat the water. And when I brung it back up to her room, she was gone, and all her clothes, too."

"Oh, dear!" exclaimed Jane, flinging back the covers and all but bounding from the bed.

"Should I tell his lordship, miss?"

"On no account!" Jane's voice was muffled somewhat by the folds of the muslin morning gown she had flung over her head. "I am sure there is quite a simple explanation, if only we—but we must not dawdle. Here, do up the back of my gown. I dare not wait for my abigail!"

Since Liza had ambitions of rising to the rarified position of lady's maid, she was nothing loth, and after fastening the back of Jane's gown and pulling her hair back and tying it with a ribbon, the two women hurried to the room Jane had assigned to Susannah.

It was empty, just as Liza had said, the bedclothes thrown back in disarray, and the curious garments Susannah had worn the day before nowhere in sight. But Jane, sweeping an appraising eye about the room, noticed a detail that Liza had missed.

"She cannot have gone far, for her valise is still here." She indicated the worn leather bag in the corner. "Is it possible that you misunderstood, and she meant to bathe after she had breakfasted?"

"Well, miss, I didn't *think* so," Liza answered cautiously. "But I suppose it's possible, what with Miss Ramsay being from America, and having odd foreign notions."

"Depend upon it, we shall discover her in the breakfast room," predicted Jane with a confidence born of desperation. "No, you need not accompany me. Only make the bed as you normally would do, and prepare the room for Miss Ramsay's return, which I daresay will be quite soon."

In spite of her reassuring words to the chambermaid, Jane could not feel entirely comfortable regarding Miss Ramsay's absence. And so instead of returning to her own room, she went downstairs to the breakfast room to look for her cousin. As she had feared, there was no sign of Miss Ramsay; in fact, Peter was the room's only occupant.

"You are up early, Cousin Jane," he noted, looking up from a plate of buttered eggs and beefsteak. Seeing distress writ large upon her usually serene countenance, he asked, "Is something wrong?"

"Oh, no—that is, I hope not, but—tell me, Peter, has Miss Ramsay been here?"

"Cousin Susannah? No."

"Oh, dear!"

He pushed his plate away and rose from the table. "What are you thinking?"

She shook her head. "To tell you the truth, I don't quite know *what* to think. She is not in her room, although Liza says she had requested water for a bath. I thought perhaps she had changed her mind, and come to breakfast first."

"Perhaps that was her intention, only she got lost on her way to the breakfast room. I very nearly did so myself, you know, when I first came to live here—more than once, in fact."

Her brow cleared at this entirely logical explanation. "Of course! How stupid of me not to have thought of it myself! I shall go in search of her at once."

"I'll help you," he said, abandoning his half-eaten beefsteak with a pang of regret. "Shall we enlist the servants? The house is rather large, you know."

"I think not," she determined after a moment's consideration. "She is bound to be embarrassed by her error, and it would not do for her to lose face in the eyes of the staff, as she is shortly to be their mistress. If you will take this floor and the cellars, I shall search the upper floors and the attics."

Peter agreed to this plan, and they set out on their separate assignments. They met in the breakfast room twenty minutes later, both shaking their heads.

"I gave the first footman a rare turn when I poked my head into his bedchamber, but I saw no sign of her anywhere," Jane recalled. "I confess, I am growing worried. What do you suppose has happened to her?"

"Perhaps she went to have a look about the grounds," Peter suggested. "If you will search the gardens about the house, I will take Sheba and ride through the Home Wood."

"Do you really think she would go so far afield?"

"You forget, I have almost two days' acquaintance with our American cousin," he reminded her with a twinkle in his eyes. "I think it is *exactly* the sort of thing she would do. Depend upon it, I shall find her in the stables, hobnobbing with the grooms."

Jane's eyebrows arched toward her hairline. "Hobnobbing with grooms? Why, pray, should she do such a thing?"

"Because it is her invariable practice. Sailors, scullery maids, no station is too humble for our Cousin Susannah to befriend."

"She sounds a very peculiar sort of girl."

"I thought so at first, but after two days in her company, I confess I find her rather charmingly unaffected." He grinned. "She is likely to give Richard more than one rare turn, however. I've never noticed that a lack of affectation was very high on his list of qualifications for a bride."

Contrary to his optimistic prediction, Susannah was not at the stables; nor, according to the head groom, had she been there all morning. So certain had been Peter's conviction that he would find her there that the wind was quite taken from his sails. Having no other alternative, he ordered Sheba saddled, and soon set out on horseback to search the farther reaches of the estate. Seeing Jane in the herb garden behind the house, he shook his head to indicate his failure, then pointed in the direction in which he intended to extend his search. Seeing her raise a hand in understanding, he nudged Sheba onward.

It was not until he rounded the corner at the far end of the house and glimpsed the broad ornamental lake beyond the trees that he had a new and disturbing thought. Surely she was not—had not—

He had not brought a riding crop—he had not thought to need one—but he slapped Sheba's flank and urged the horse into a gallop. The lake was beautiful, but its banks were quite steep in places, and it was deeper than the unwary might suppose. Sure enough, as he drew nearer, he saw a dark head bobbing just above the surface of the water. Flinging himself from the saddle, he ran the last few steps, shedding his coat and waistcoat and tossing them aside as he slid down the grassy bank.

"Susannah, I'm coming! I'm—"

She turned at the sound of his voice, and the words died on his lips. Far from drowning, she stood at a depth of about four feet, her head and shoulders breaking the surface of the lake. Streams of water ran from her hair, trembling in diamond-like drops from the ends of each curl, spilling over bare shoulders, and running in rivulets down the slight indentation that narrowed into the crevice between her—

Crimson faced, Peter fixed his gaze determinedly on her face. "What the devil are you doing?" His breath came in laboured gasps that had little to do with his recent exertions.

"I'm taking a bath," she explained, as if bathing naked in an ornamental lake were the most natural thing in the world.

"Are you aware that the whole household is searching for you?" he demanded with less than perfect truth. "Come out of there at once! No, wait! Don't!" She showed no sign of obeying this behest, but Peter, taking no chances, held up a hand as if to forestall her.

"Give me my towel," she said.

"What—? Where—?"

She raised one dripping arm to point. "Right there. Behind you."

He turned, and saw what he had not noticed before. A thick white towel hung from the branch of a tree, as did her coarse skirt and bodice. Peter silently blessed the long-ago Lord Ramsay who had commissioned no less a personage than Capability Brown to design the lake and its surrounding grounds; the trees which the famed landscaper had instructed to be planted along this side of the water were now the only thing that kept the entire household from getting to know the next Lady Ramsay a great deal too well.

Peter plucked the towel from its branch and edged down the bank as near to the water as he dared, then manfully turned his back and held the towel out at arm's length behind him. A splashing sound informed him that Susannah was emerging from her bath, and he ruthlessly suppressed a mental image of Aphrodite rising naked from the sea. A moment later the towel was plucked from his hand. Without looking back, he climbed the bank, picking up his coat and waistcoat along the way, and cringing at the thought of how this perfectly innocent activity must look to any interested observer. By the time Susannah climbed the sloping ground to join him, he had donned both garments and now made himself very busy with the horse's saddle and bridle.

"I didn't mean to worry anyone," she said apologetically. "But Liza asked me if I wanted to take a bath, and I told her that I did."

"She meant that, if you were ready, she would bring hot water for you." Steeling himself, he turned away from the horse to regard his errant cousin. He was relieved to find her fully (if unfashionably) dressed, the only sign of her recent infraction being the occasional drop of water that still fell from the ends of her hair. "Surely you have had a hot bath before!"

"Well, yes, in the winter. But in the summer months, it is so much easier to go down to the river to bathe. After all, why go to the trouble of lighting a fire and heating water when—"

"Cousin Susannah," he interrupted ruthlessly, "let me remind you that we have servants here, servants who are well paid for 'going to the trouble,' as you say, of doing the work they were engaged to do!"

"I—I'm sorry. I didn't think—I'm not accustomed to having people do for me, you know. I won't do it again."

He sighed, relenting. "I suppose there's no harm done. Still, we'd best get you back to the house before Richard finds out."

He started to offer her a boost into the saddle, then had a sudden vision of Lady Godiva riding through the streets of Coventry, and thought better of it. Instead, he looped the reins over Sheba's head and, taking Susannah by the elbow, led the horse with one hand and his cousin with the other as they made their way first to the stables and thence to the house.

6

Beware of all enterprises that require new clothes.
HENRY DAVID THOREAU, *Walden*

*T*hank God you found her before Richard did!"
exclaimed Jane, clapping a hand to her
forehead in dismay.

Susannah had been dispatched to her own room
where she might dry her hair before the fire, leaving
Peter to recount to Jane in privacy the story of how he
had discovered her bathing in the lake.

"Yes, I'm sure it was very fortunate, my coming
along when I did," Peter said thoughtfully. "And yet I
wonder—"

Given Richard's apparent indifference toward his
chosen bride, it might have done him a great deal of
good to have seen her as Peter had, emerging from the
lake like a naiad, with water streaming from her hair
and over her bare shoulders. The picture she presented

might have gone a long way toward shaking Richard out of his apathy; certainly the image was one Peter would not easily forget.

"Yes?" Jane prompted. "What do you wonder?"

He shook his head, dismissing the thought, if not the image. "Nothing really, only—Cousin Jane, do you think—does it occur to you that perhaps Richard is making a mistake?"

She sighed. "Yes, frequently! And never more so than last night, when he mistook his chosen bride for a serving girl. But you know what he is, Peter. He sees his duty clear, and he would not go back on his word, were she ten times more ineligible." She smiled rather wistfully. "It is one of his more admirable qualities, even though it does make one occasionally long to box his ears."

"Do you think they can be happy together?"

"I suppose it depends upon how willing they are to adjust their expectations of one another. I have reason to believe that Susannah may not be as hopeless a case as Richard seems to fear, for as I pointed out to him, she is already accustomed to running a household, albeit a very different one."

"Yes, and she certainly came the great lady when she believed him to be deliberately insulting her, did she not?" Peter agreed, grinning at the memory. "I confess, for that one brief moment I had no difficulty at all in seeing her as Lady Ramsay."

"Yes, indeed! So I think we must try to be charitable, and mark the bath incident down to ignorance. And, as the best antidote to ignorance is instruction, I shall take her over the house as soon as may be arranged, and explain to her what will be her duties as the next Lady Ramsay. I had hoped to take her to my dressmaker this afternoon, but I suppose that must wait until tomorrow."

Peter's brow puckered in a thoughtful frown. "I am sure you know best, Cousin Jane, but won't it take several days to have dresses made up?"

"Oh, yes—days, if not weeks."

"In that case, would you not do better to let the dressmaking visit stand, and postpone the tour of the house until tomorrow?"

"I suppose so," Jane agreed somewhat reluctantly. With a hint of a smile, she added, "We shall only hope that our American cousin will stay out of the lake in the meantime."

With this Parthian shot, she left the room, determined to seek out Susannah before her baser self could compose a compelling argument as to why delaying Susannah's transformation into a young lady of fashion would be the wisest course of action.

* * *

Susannah, for her part, remained in her room only until her hair had dried sufficiently to tie it back with a ribbon (from which, no doubt, it would soon escape) before making her way downstairs to the drawing room—this chamber being, with the exceptions of the dining room and her own bedchamber, the only room of the house with which she was acquainted.

Having reached her destination and congratulated herself for finding it without assistance, she entered the room only to find Lord Ramsay there before her.

"Oh!" she exclaimed, startled. "I had not thought— I did not mean to interrupt, my lord."

He laid aside his newspaper and rose to greet her. "Nonsense! In fact, I am pleased to see you, Cousin Susannah." He cleared his throat. "I believe I owe you an apology."

"No apology is necessary, Lord Ramsay," she said, inclining her head with a formality that matched his own.

"I beg to differ. In any case, I hope you will indulge me by accepting it, and by calling me Richard or, if that seems too familiar on such short acquaintance, Cousin Richard." He smiled fleetingly, and she was surprised to discover that his smile was surprisingly sweet. "I assure you, however formal our

English ways must appear to you, we do draw the line at requiring a woman to call her husband by his title."

Her answering smile was somewhat tentative. "Very well—Cousin Richard."

"Peter tells me you are fond of riding. I hope you will allow me to show you about the property tomorrow. I would propose this afternoon for the excursion, but Jane tells me she intends to take you to her dressmaker immediately after luncheon. It would be a very odd female, I believe, who would prefer an hour in the saddle to one spent shopping for frills and furbelows."

"Really?" Susannah regarded him with mild curiosity. "Why?"

"My dear cousin," he said, exasperated, "surely you cannot expect me to explain to you the peculiar joy which members of your sex seem to find in debating the virtues of silk over satin, or finding the perfect shade of ribbon to match one's new gown!"

"I'm afraid *someone* must, for I've never done either of those things. Nor have I ever shopped for— what did you say?—frills or furbelows. What exactly *is* a furbelow, anyway?"

He held up his hands in mock surrender. "I'm afraid you are asking the wrong person, my dear. You would do better to direct your questions to Jane."

"There is one other thing, my lord—er, Cousin Richard. How much will all this cost? You know I am accounted a considerable heiress back home, but most of my assets are in land. I haven't that much available as ready money."

He shook his head. "The cost need not concern you. I will cover any expenditure."

"No, you will not!" exclaimed Susannah, much shocked. "I may be an American, but even in America we know better than to let a man buy clothing, or—or anything of an intimate nature—for a woman who is not his wife!"

"Not *yet* his wife," he amended. "Let me remind you that in addition to being your betrothed, I am also your cousin. No matter how distant the blood tie, I am still the head of your family, and no one will think it in the least unusual for me to see that you are properly outfitted. Indeed, it would be thought very shabby of me to do otherwise."

Susannah was not at all certain whether to trust him on this but, having no other choice in the matter, elected to let the matter drop until she might put the question to her cousin Jane. In truth, she found Cousin Jane's quiet elegance rather intimidating. Seated beside her in the carriage, Susannah felt decidedly frumpy, never suspecting that Jane had chosen her own rather sober carriage dress in order to diminish, as much as possible, the difference in her own attire and that of her American cousin.

"I hope you will find this enjoyable," Jane said brightly, as they set out. "I well remember when the Dowager Lady Ramsay—Richard's mother, that is— engaged me as her companion, and brought me to Madame Lavert to be outfitted. I was quite poor, you know, and had little besides the clothes on my back. I felt like Cinderella!"

Susannah returned a mechanical smile, but her thoughts were elsewhere. "Miss Hawthorne—"

"Cousin Jane," corrected that lady.

"Cousin Jane, then, my lord—that is, Cousin Richard intends to pay for any clothing I buy. Is that— well, is it quite proper?"

"I assure you, Richard would not offer to do such a thing if there were anything untoward in it. He is very aware of his position, you know—as well as yours— and would do nothing that might expose you to scandal or censure. You may be easy on that head."

In fact, it had been Lord Ramsay who had insisted that the ladies take the closed carriage for the short drive to the village, thus denying the villages the opportunity to gawk at the future Lady Ramsay before he was ready to present her to them. Still, the sight of the baronial carriage, its door emblazoned with the family crest, was enough to evoke inquisitive glances from the villagers, whose curiosity was rewarded by a glimpse of unruly red curls and a *retroussé* nose pressed to the glass.

The village of Lower Nettleby was fortunate in its dressmaker, for Madame Lavert, having fled Paris at the height of the Terror after losing most of her noble clients to the guillotine, had been left with so violent a dislike for large cities that she had eschewed London and settled instead in this rural corner of Hampshire. A birdlike little woman with a sharp chin and a pointed nose, she now enjoyed the patronage of a limited yet lucrative clientele. Upon being introduced to Susannah, she fingered that young lady's coarse skirts and unfashionable cotton bodice while declaiming in voluble French, the only words of which Susannah understood were *"l'Américaine gauche."*

At the end of this tirade, she addressed Susannah with a flurry of hand gestures, directing her to the small room at the rear of the shop, where she might disrobe. After allowing her new client sufficient time for this operation, she descended upon her with a dressmaker's tape, with which (it seemed to Susannah) she measured every part of her body which she might conceivably wish to cover with clothing. Having made careful note of these calculations, she at last stepped back and informed Susannah that she might put her clothes back on, although the tone of her voice and the Gallic twist of her lip suggested her own doubts as to why anyone would wish to do so.

After Susannah dressed (wondering, as Lord Ramsay had, why any female should find such an ordeal enjoyable), she joined her cousin and the dressmaker in the main room of the shop where, to her surprise, she heard the little Frenchwoman praising her, albeit with compliments of the left-handed variety.

"*La petite Américaine*, she has not mademoiselle's own elegance of form, but she is, what do you say, pleasingly proportioned, and round in all the right places. *Oui*, I can make something of her. Not a beauty, *non*, but an Original—something out of the common way. But—" She wagged a finger in front of Jane's nose. "You must do something about the hair, *oui*? Else all my *travail*, he is for naught."

"Yes, we will certainly have Miss Ramsay's hair coiffed," Jane promised. "I had thought to send for Miss Williams—"

"Bah! *That* for Miss Williams!" exclaimed Madame Lavert, snapping her fingers at the mention of Jane's own hairdresser."

"She has always done quite well with my hair—"

86

Jane protested.

"But yes, with *your* hair. My kitchen maid could style your hair, and she is half blind. But Mademoiselle Ramsay's hair—" Taking one of the escaped curls between her thumb and forefinger, she pulled it straight and then released it. She frowned as it sprang back into its original corkscrew shape. "Mademoiselle Ramsay's hair requires something different, *oui*? You must send for my nephew, Claude Lavert."

"Send for him? Where is he?"

"He is in London, where he has a shop in Piccadilly."

Susannah, tired of being spoken of as if she were not there, clasped both hands to her offensive curls. "London? I cannot possibly go all the way to London for a haircut!"

Madame Lavert turned to regard Susannah as if she had only that moment remembered her presence. "Go to London?" she echoed. "But of course you must not go to London! My nephew must wait upon you at Ramsay Hall."

"It seems a lot of trouble—" protested Susannah, only to be silenced by a look from Jane.

"Thank you for the recommendation, Madame. I will certainly speak to Lord Ramsay on the subject. Now we should like to see fashion plates and fabric samples, if you please."

"*Mais oui!* A moment, *s'il vous plaît.*" She darted behind the counter, and when she returned, her arms were laden with books. She set the pile on the table with a thud, and removed the first volume from the top of the pile. "First we will look at the dresses, *oui*?"

And what dresses they were! Susannah, who had never at any time in her life owned more than two changes of clothing, was quite overwhelmed with the variety of garments that Madame Lavert and Cousin Jane considered necessary for a lady's wardrobe. There were morning gowns and afternoon gowns for day wear, with long sleeves and high necklines; dinner gowns and evening dresses with tiny puffed sleeves and abbreviated bodices that displayed shocking expanses of bosom; and cloaks, spencers, and pelisses for out-of-doors, trimmed in braid and fastened with frogs.

Here, however, Susannah was moved to protest. "I don't need a coat. I already have one."

Madame Lavert regarded the fringed buckskin monstrosity with a contemptuous curl of her lip. "This? You would prefer *this* over Madame Lavert's genius? Better you should put it on the fire."

"I won't!" Susannah declared mulishly, hugging the garment about her as if fearful the little Frenchwoman might attempt to remove it by force. "It was my father's."

"Then of course you must keep it," Jane agreed. "Still, you will want to take good care of it. If you had a cloak and perhaps a pelisse, you would not be obliged to expose your father's coat to inclement weather."

The dressmaker bristled at the suggestion that her own creations were more expendable than the contemptible buckskin garment, but a speaking look from Jane silenced any protest she might have been inclined to make. Susannah was forced to concede the wisdom of this argument, and the tense moment passed.

Next came the fabric samples. Madame Lavert placed a small looking glass before Susannah, and that rather bemused young lady stared dazedly at her own reflection as Madame draped folds of cloth across her chest from shoulder to shoulder, the better to study the effects of Pomona green silk as opposed to peach-colored satin. Susannah, noting with amazement the effects of these miraculous materials upon a face she had hitherto considered quite ordinary, realized that this was the process to which Lord Ramsay had referred. She decided that it was really quite pleasurable, after all. As Madame Lavert gauged the effect of a celestial blue lutestring, Susannah decided she enjoyed it very much indeed.

"I—I should like something pink, if you please,"

whispered Susannah, finding her voice at last.

"Pink?" echoed Jane in some consternation. "My dear cousin, with your coloring, I don't think—"

Madame Lavert took Susannah's chin in her hand and studied her face intently. "Not rose, *non*. But the very palest hue—" She rummaged through the pile of fabrics, and finally unearthed the one she sought. She arranged it across Susannah's bosom and stepped back to gauge the effect. "*Voilà!*"

"Oh!" breathed Susannah, wide-eyed.

" 'Oh,' indeed," agreed Jane, noting with mixed emotions the creamy ivory of the girl's skin and the fiery highlights in her hair. "Madame, Miss Ramsay will need the other dresses first, but you must certainly use this to make up her gown for the ball."

"B-Ball?" All Susannah's pleasure evaporated, leaving in its place a cold lump of dread.

"Has his lordship not told you? How very like him! Of course there will be a ball to introduce you formally to the neighborhood gentry." Seeing panic writ large upon her cousin's expressive countenance, she hastened to reassure her. "It will not be for several weeks yet. By that time, I daresay you shall feel as if you have lived here all your life."

Jane next inquired of Madame as to undergarments, which proved to be petticoats, shifts, stays, and even the new pantalettes, all made of lawn and batiste of so fine a weave as to be almost transparent. As disturbing as it was to think of her remote cousin Richard seeing her in such intimate apparel (much less out of it), still more terrifying to Susannah's mind was the prospect of the ball at which she, clad in a cloud of palest pink gauze, would demonstrate her ignorance to the world.

"Miss Hawthorne—" she began, once they had left the dressmaker's shop and were safely ensconced in the closed carriage.

"Cousin Jane," that lady reminded her, smiling.

"Cousin Jane, then, about this ball—must I—that is, will I be expected to dance?"

"My dear Cousin Susannah, you will be the guest of honour! It would look very odd if, after the betrothal is announced, you and Richard did not dance together."

"It would look even odder if we did," Susannah muttered miserably.

"I beg your pardon?"

"I can't dance," she said with the guilty air of one confessing to the most heinous of crimes. "I've never learned how."

"I see," said Jane, momentarily daunted. "I confess, it had never occurred to me that—but I can see that dancing masters must have been in short supply on the

American frontier. Well then, we shall just have to teach you."

"Surely you cannot mean to send to London for a dancing master as well as a hairdresser!"

"No, for as it is the height of the Season, I doubt we could persuade one to leave London at a time when their services are bound to be in demand. But *we* could teach you, Richard and I, with Aunt Amelia providing music on the pianoforte."

"Surely Lord Ramsay—that is, Cousin Richard— must have better things to do than to—to prance around the ballroom giving dancing lessons!"

Jane's lips twitched at the idea of Lord Ramsay "prancing" anywhere, but she merely said, "If he cannot spare us an hour or two in the afternoon, we shall enlist Peter's help instead."

Susannah, somewhat mollified, nodded in agreement. If it occurred to her to wonder why this suggestion should be so much more acceptable than Jane's first proposal, she gave no outward sign.

7

Here's to the housewife that's thrifty.
RICHARD BRINSLEY SHERIDAN,
The School for Scandal

*A*s the first of Susannah's new gowns would not be ready for several days, Jane determined to alter one of her own dresses to fit her cousin. The selection of a suitable dress proved to be quite a challenge, since Susannah was (as Madame Lavert had noted) both shorter and curvier than her English counterpart. She finally settled on a simple lilac gown of figured muslin with a drawstring fastening beneath the bosom which might be adjusted to accommodate Susannah's somewhat rounder form. The length, too, could be shortened by the simple expedient of removing the flounce adorning the hem.

Susannah, much moved by this gesture, protested her unworthiness of such a sacrifice, but seeing that Jane would not be gainsaid, at least determined to spare her the labour by performing the necessary alterations herself.

"Oh, can you sew?" Jane asked, heartened by this hint of hidden talents on Susannah's part.

"Not like you do," the younger girl confessed, glancing wistfully at Jane's embroidery in its tambour frame. "That is, I've never done fine needlework, but *someone* had to darn the stockings and sew the loose buttons on Papa's shirts and, well, that someone was me."

"Excellent!" pronounced Jane. "My sewing basket should contain everything you require, but if you cannot find some article you need, you have only to ask."

Susannah promised to do so, and then set to work—the end result being that, when the family assembled for luncheon, she was very creditably gowned, even if her hair was its usual unruly self.

Peter, upon seeing his erstwhile charge's borrowed plumes, was moved to exclaim, "Very nice, Cousin Susannah. Does she not look well, Richard?"

Lord Ramsay, seeing some expression of approval on his part was expected, bent a smile upon his betrothed, said, "Yes, much better," and took his place at the head of the table. Seeing the scowl Jane directed at him, and quite misinterpreting its meaning, he added,

"I need not ask whom to credit for the improvement, Susannah, for I detect the hand of our Cousin Jane at work. I hope you remembered to thank her for her kindness."

"If you detected *my* hand at work, Richard, I fear your eyesight is failing," put in Jane, with a smile for her American cousin. "In fact, it was Cousin Susannah's needlework, not mine, that deserves the credit—while as for her thanking me, do not, I beg you, set her off again! It was only with the greatest difficulty that I persuaded her that she would in fact be doing me a service in relieving me of a gown that never flattered me above half."

This last was quite untrue, as the gown in question had been delivered from Madame Lavert's hands only a fortnight earlier, and had quickly become one of Jane's favourites. Still, it was the only garment she owned which might have served the purpose, and so nothing could be gained by regrets on her part, or further expressions of gratitude on Susannah's.

"My mistake," Richard acknowledged with a nod, then turned his attention back to his betrothed. "So tell me, Susannah, what did you think of your first visit to a dressmaker's shop?"

This conversational gambit was considerably more successful. Susannah's expressive blue eyes lit with enthusiasm, and she launched into a description of the morning's adventures that doubtlessly bored the gentlemen very much, but gave Richard the opportunity to observe, as Peter had already noticed, that Susannah Ramsay, when animated, was surprisingly attractive in spite of the unfortunate hair and freckles.

"Am I to understand, then, that you preferred this activity to riding after all?"

Susannah's brow puckered as she considered the question. "No, I can't say I *preferred* it, exactly, for they are two such different things are they not?"

"You relieve my mind," Richard said. "While I hope to share some common amusements with my wife, I do draw the line at shopping together for ribbons and laces."

Susannah blushed and giggled at the thought of the very masculine Lord Ramsay invading Madame Lavert's decidedly feminine establishment. Jane, observing this promising reaction, pressed one hand to a heart that clenched painfully at the first sign of rapport between the lord of the manor and his chosen bride.

"Of course, Susannah has not yet had the pleasure of submitting her head to be coiffed," Jane put in hastily, to cover her own anguish. "Madame Lavert urged me to have you send to London for her nephew,

Monsieur Claude Lavert."

"Then we must do so, by all means." Richard's ready agreement, though upon closer examination hardly flattering to Susannah, was graciousness itself.

"I hope he can be persuaded to leave London at the height of the Season," fretted Jane.

"I can see that I must make it worth his while to tear himself away." He turned to Peter. "Pay whatever he asks, and make it clear that I will cover the expense of his travel on the Royal Mail."

Peter acknowledged this command with a nod and, as soon as he had finished luncheon, took himself off to the small, sunny room on the ground floor which served as his office in order to carry out these instructions. Richard soon excused himself as well, and Jane, left alone with Susannah, smiled at her across the table.

"If you have finished, Cousin Susannah, I had thought to show you about the house this afternoon, and to introduce you to its staff."

Susannah, willing if not eager, consented to this plan, and the two ladies left the dining room and descended the stairs that led to the servants' domain. Here she was introduced first to the housekeeper, Mrs. Meeks.

"Mrs. Meeks, you must know, is the head of all the female staff," Jane explained. "You will consult with her once a week, and more frequently if there are unusual issues that need to be addressed—overnight guests who need to be accommodated, for instance, or the hiring of extra staff for large entertainments."

"Like—like the betrothal ball?" asked Susannah.

"Aye, miss, like the betrothal ball." The housekeeper beamed at her future mistress's ready understanding. "But strictly speaking, you won't be my Lady Ramsay yet, so you need not take a hand in the planning of it unless you've a liking to. The same goes for the wedding breakfast, as I'm sure Miss Hawthorne will agree."

"Yes, of course," Jane concurred, forcing herself to keep smiling at the prospect of being obliged to organize this celebration of the death of her own hopes. "Still, you might like to help with the arrangements, just to learn how such things are done." Not wishing to diminish the new mistress in the eyes of her staff, Jane explained for the housekeeper's benefit, "Miss Ramsay has had the charge of her father's house from a young age, but it was not so large as this one."

Mrs. Meeks accepted this masterpiece of understatement without question. "Aye, and it being in America, I don't doubt their ways were different from ours. Depend upon it, miss, I'll do anything I can to help you adjust, and I think I can say the same for the whole staff, except for—tell me, Miss Hawthorne, does—that is, has Miss Ramsay met Antoine yet?"

Jane grimaced. "No, that pleasure still awaits her." To Susannah she added, "Antoine, the chef—pray *don't* call him a cook, whatever you do!—is a French *émigré*, as his name suggests. He is a genius in the kitchen, but is a bit temperamental."

"More than a bit!" Mrs. Meeks put in emphatically. "He's a regular tyrant in the kitchen, but never you mind. Miss Hawthorne here knows just how to handle him, and I don't doubt she'll show you the way of it."

"The secret is flattery, no more nor less," confided Jane, laughing. "Fortunately, his accomplishments in the kitchen make it easy to heap on compliments without the least hint of hypocrisy. Then, after you have emptied the butter boat over his head, you may approach the issue that must be addressed, making it clear that you are fully aware of the sacrifice you are asking of poor Antoine, obliged as he is to live in a world populated by mere mortals."

"He sounds quite insufferable!" exclaimed Susannah, appalled.

"Oh, he is. But when you have sampled a meal of his creation—for last night's cannot be said to count, as I wrecked all his plans by moving dinner forward upon Lord Ramsay's arrival—you will see why he is to be indulged at all costs. Indeed, his lordship would be most displeased if you were to provoke Antoine to give notice."

With these words of warning, Jane led the way to the kitchen, where she was introduced not only to Antoine, but to the army of underlings who apparently jumped at his beck and call, from the middle-aged woman who served as undercook to the ten-year-old pot boy who regarded the Frenchman with an air of awe not unmixed with abject terror.

"Once a week you will consult with Antoine over the week's meals, so that he may plan his marketing accordingly," Jane explained while the culinary genius and his future mistress eyed one another warily. "In fact, I intend to make out a menu later this afternoon. Why don't you plan one of this week's dinners yourself, and add it to my list? It will be good practice for you, and Antoine can begin to learn your preferences."

After her initial meeting with the tyrant of the kitchen, the rest of the staff, including the male contingent under the dominion of Wilson, the butler, held no power to terrify. It was not until later, when Jane gave the unfinished menu to her with instructions that she make her own additions before sending it downstairs to Antoine by way of the footman, that something approaching panic set in.

"But—but what shall I write?"

"Whatever you wish to eat," Jane said, thinking, no doubt, to be reassuring. "Whatever cannot be found in Richard's own succession houses will be purchased at the village market."

"Succession houses?" echoed Susannah, unfamiliar with the term.

"You must have him show them to you on your ride tomorrow. "Oranges, grapes, peaches—anything that will not grow in the natural climate thrives in abundance in the succession houses." She glanced down at the unfinished list in Susannah's hand. "As for the menu, why, you must have done something similar when you kept house for your father, even if you did not write it down. What was your father's favourite meal? You might wish to begin with that."

After Jane had gone, leaving her cousin alone with this task, Susannah tapped the pencil against her cheek and studied the paper in her hand. There in Jane's neat hand were transcribed each evening's meal: roast beef cooked in port wine sauce, potatoes with rosemary, and buttered peas; chicken with mushroom gravy, to be served over rice, and carrots with slivered almonds . . .

While meals on their Kentucky homestead were largely dependent on the season, there were apparently no such restrictions here. How, then, was one to know where to begin? *What was your father's favourite meal?* Jane had suggested. It seemed as good an idea as any other. Taking a deep breath, Susannah set pencil to paper and began to write. A few minutes later, she laid the pencil aside and folded the paper in half, then tugged the bell pull and, ignoring the butterflies cavorting about her stomach, gave the folded paper to the footman along with instructions that it was to be delivered to Antoine.

Thus was her first act as lady of the manor accomplished.

* * *

While Susannah made out her menu, Richard regarded Jane across the chessboard set up in the drawing room.

"Well, Jane?"

She looked up from contemplation of her next move. " 'Well' what?"

"You might as well tell me what I have done to earn your displeasure. You have given me such quelling looks since luncheon that I am shaking in my boots."

"Yes, I can see that, for your play is slipping," she said, and took his bishop.

He scowled at this unexpected act of aggression on her part. "Hmm, if I had been paying closer attention, I should have captured that pawn before you could commit such an atrocity. Still, I trust you are going to enlighten me as to my transgressions?"

"I wonder that I should have to," she said, torn between exasperation and amusement. " 'Much better'? Was that the best you could do?"

"My dear Jane, what are you talking about?" he asked, all at sea.

"Richard! Can you have already forgotten? I am speaking of Cousin Susannah, and her appearance at luncheon!"

"What of it? I paid her a compliment, did I not?"

"*Peter* paid her a compliment; *you* merely indicated that her earlier appearance had left much to be desired."

He stared at her, utterly baffled by her argument. "Can you truly mean to suggest that it did not?"

"Of course not! But it was unhandsome of you to point it out."

"I did no such thing! I merely stated that I found her appearance improved—which is true. Surely there can be no objection to that!"

"I don't *object*, precisely, but I do think you might have—"

Alas, Lord Ramsay was deprived of the opportunity to benefit from this advice by the arrival of Antoine, who burst into the room unannounced and uninvited. That he was labouring under some strong emotion was immediately obvious, not only by this unheard-of breach of etiquette, but also by the Frenchman's countenance (which was of so dark a red hue as to be almost purple) and by the shaking hand that thrust a folded paper under Jane's nose.

"*Sacre bleu!* It is an insult not to be borne!"

"It must be, for you to force your presence on us in this fashion," Jane said coldly.

"*Mille pardons, mademoiselle,* but this—this—" He shook the paper in her face. "I will give notice before I so demean myself and my Art!"

She snatched the paper from his trembling hand, spread the sheet, and choked. There were her own instructions for the week's meals and, below, an addition in an unfamiliar hand: *squirrel fried in lard,* Susannah had written, *with cornmeal mush.*

"I gather Miss Ramsay's dinner choices do not please you," she addressed the offended chef in a voice that quivered only slightly.

"Do not please me? *Do not please me?*"

"Let me remind you, Antoine, that Miss Ramsay is shortly to become Lady Ramsay. As such, she will expect her orders to be obeyed."

"*Très bon!* In that case, *mademoiselle,* I will give notice at once."

She inclined a regal head in acknowledgement. "We will miss you, and wish you well in your future endeavors."

"*Mais non!* I will slit my throat before I defile my kitchen with this—this—"

"Thank you for informing us," replied Jane, unmoved. "We will be sure to send flowers."

"*Cette insulte*, she is *insupportable!*" continued the Frenchman, still in full flow.

"I know this is not what you are accustomed to, Antoine, but let me point out that Miss Ramsay is but recently arrived from the American frontier. She will learn our ways, but in the meantime, is it really so much to ask, to let her have her way this once? Surely you, of all people, must know what it is like, to be obliged to leave all that is familiar and start anew in a strange land." Seeing his angry color begin to fade, she lowered her eyes demurely to the chessboard. "But I can see I am asking too much of you. No one could possibly do anything with such a meal plan as this."

The Frenchman drew himself up straight as a ramrod. " 'No one,' *mademoiselle*? Perhaps 'no one' could, but then, Antoine is not 'no one'! I, Antoine, can do what others cannot—as you shall see this very night!" With this promise (or was it a threat?), he grabbed the paper from her hand and quitted the room in high dudgeon.

Richard, who had listened to this exchange in silence, now regarded his cousin Jane with unconcealed admiration. "My dear Jane! I never until this moment suspected that behind that pretty face lies a master manipulator. Well done, indeed! Dare I ask what our American cousin has in store for us that so lacerated Antoine's delicate sensibilities?"

"I think I will let you discover it for yourself, when we sit down to dinner," she said, blushing a little at the unexpected compliment. "I confess, I am curious to see what he will do with it."

"Very well, keep your secrets. Still, I can't help but wonder on how many occasions you have managed me just as successfully, and I never suspected a thing."

She gave him a mysterious smile. "I'll never tell."

"In that case, there is only one thing to be said."

"And what is that, Richard?"

"Checkmate," he replied, and slid his queen across the board.

* * *

And so it was that, when the family sat down to dinner that night, they were served by a grinning footman bearing a platter containing half a dozen cutlets encased in a golden brown crust, all resting on a bed of parsley adorned at intervals by radishes cleverly carved to resemble roses. Behind him, the second footman carried a large plate of some pale substance molded into a ring, the center cavity of which was filled with an assortment of grapes, cherries, and plums.

"Oh!" breathed Susannah when this masterpiece was placed before her. "Antoine *is* a genius!"

"Monsieur Antoine begs mademoiselle's pardon, Miss Ramsay, but he took the liberty of substituting butter for the, er, lard," confided the footman offering the platter.

"What the devil is this?" demanded Richard as one of the breaded cutlets was transferred from the platter to his plate.

"Squirrel, my lord," replied the footman, struggling to keep his countenance. "Or, as Monsieur Antoine calls it, *Écureuil au beurre.*"

"And that?" Richard's voice rose ominously as he nodded toward the plate with the ring mold.

"Er, corn meal 'mush,' my lord," the second footman said apologetically. "Or, if you prefer, '*cirque de farine avec fruites.*' " He pronounced the French words as if they had been dutifully committed to memory—which, indeed, they had, him having no French of his own at his command.

"If I *prefer*?" echoed Lord Ramsay, dumbfounded. "What I *prefer* is—is—" His gaze shifted from his betrothed's glowing countenance to Jane's pleading one, beseeching him from her place at the opposite end of the table. "What I prefer is that you should carry my compliments to Monsieur Antoine, along with Miss Ramsay's."

He returned Jane's grateful smile with a rather sheepish one of his own, then picked up his fork.

8

He's a wonderful talker, who has the art
of telling you nothing in a great harangue.
MOLIÈRE, *Le Misanthrope*

The following morning, Lord Ramsay arose betimes and dressed carefully in a russet-colored riding coat, buckskin breeches, and top boots; today he was to go riding with his betrothed, and he was determined that Jane should not accuse him of being backward in any attention. He made his way down the stairs toward the breakfast room, idly slapping his riding crop against his boot, but upon reaching this sunny chamber, he was informed by the butler that Miss Ramsay had been there before him. He thanked Wilson for the information, then made a quick repast before setting out for the stables.

Or at least, such was his intention. But as he crossed the hall, he glanced toward the window, and the sight framed in the elegantly arched aperture was sufficient to make him revise his plans for the morning. A female with a basket of flowers on her arm stood there on the edge of the raked gravel drive, and although the wide brim of her gypsy hat hid her face from him, he recognized her at once as his cousin Jane. She was apparently deep in conversation with Sir Matthew Pitney but, knowing her as he did, Richard could not fail to notice the way she turned slightly away from Sir Matthew as if impatient to return to the house. Nor had he any difficulty in interpreting the shake of her head as a firm refusal to allow the middle-aged baronet to carry her basket. Alas, these cues, so obvious to Lord Ramsay even from a distance were utterly lost on Sir Matthew, who showed no signs of taking "no" for an answer.

"Devil take it," muttered Richard, and crossed the hall to fling open the door of the small room which served as the steward's office.

Peter sat within, carefully entering neat rows of figures into the estate ledger, but he looked up when his cousin and employer intruded upon his work.

"Peter, I fear I must ask a favour." He glanced at the open ledger on the desk. "I hope this is not a bad time?"

"Not at all," lied Peter, stifling a sigh as he returned the quill to its stand and mentally calculating how many hours of work he had lost since Miss Susannah Ramsay had descended upon them. "What can I do for you?"

"That prosy old bore, Pitney, is here, and I won't have him badgering Jane with prying questions about Miss Ramsay."

"Will he do so? I wasn't aware that Sir Matthew had any interest in Miss Ramsay," Peter observed. "In any case, Jane has never had any difficulty before in putting him in his place when the need arose."

"Perhaps not, but depend upon it, he will lose no opportunity to press his suit with her, and I'll not allow him to fill her head with visions of becoming an unpaid drudge to my wife. But the devil's in it that I am promised to take Susannah riding."

"I see." Peter pushed back his chair and rose to his feet. "You want me to rescue Cousin Jane from his clutches? I shall be happy to do so."

"Actually, I would prefer that you take Susannah riding," Richard confessed, conscious of a vague feeling of embarrassment, although he was uncertain as to why this should be so. "Sir Matthew is oblivious to hints, and you are a great deal too diplomatic to suit the purpose. An admirable trait, I'm sure, but it renders you singularly unsuitable for dealing with Sir Matthew."

Peter grinned, taking this criticism in the spirit in

which it was intended. "Very well, but would it not be better just to postpone your ride until after Sir Matthew is gone?"

Richard had the grace to look ashamed. "Perhaps, but I confess I would prefer to have Miss Ramsay well away from the house for the duration of his visit. He is as gossipy as an old woman, you know, and it wouldn't do for him to make her acquaintance until she is fit to be presented."

"Very well, then, I shall change clothes and meet her at the stables directly." He started for the door, then paused as a new thought occurred to him. "I should think Daffodil would do for her, don't you?"

"My thoughts exactly. Daffy is the most docile creature in the stables. Susannah should have no difficulty in handling her."

Peter nodded in agreement, then took himself off to don his riding clothes.

* * *

Susannah, in the meantime, faced a dilemma of her own. When she had dressed that morning, she had put on the same lilac muslin that Jane had given her the day before, correctly assuming that she would be expected to wear this until Madame Lavert should deliver the first of her new gowns. It was not until she had reached the stables that she discovered this costume, although undeniably more attractive than her own garments, was eminently unsuited for riding. Its skirts were much too narrow to allow her to hook her knee over the pommel of the sidesaddle without hitching them up so high as to be almost indecent. Too late, she realized that, of all the gowns discussed at length in the Frenchwoman's shop, there had been no mention of riding attire. She glanced toward the stable door. Lord Ramsay (really, she must at least *try* to think of him as Richard!) would arrive at any minute; she did not want to keep him waiting, and still less did she want to bombard him with questions regarding ladies' riding clothes which he might be ill-equipped to answer in any case.

She looked down at her straight skirts and sighed. There was only one thing to do. She stooped and took the hem of her borrowed gown firmly in both hands.

* * *

Peter arrived at the stables a short time later, having hastily changed into an olive green riding coat, fawn-coloured breeches, and top boots. Had he been in less of a hurry, he might have noticed the coterie of grinning stable hands who steadfastly refused to meet his eye.

"Cousin Richard sends his apologies, Susannah, but he—Good God!" He drew up short at the sight of his American cousin standing beside Sheba's stall and stroking the horse's velvety nose. Susannah wore the same muslin gown she'd altered the day before, with one new modification: the side seams of the dress had been ripped open from hemline to hip. "What—what happened to you?"

"I couldn't possibly ride in it any other way," she pointed out reasonably.

"You can't possibly ride in it *now!* Go back to the house at once and—no, wait," he amended hastily, recalling the presence of Sir Matthew Pitney. "Come with me. I'll take you back to the house by way of a side entrance, so no one will see you."

The sound of muffled laughter somewhere behind him reminded him of the presence of the stable hands. "No one *else* will see you, anyway. And if anyone is inclined to gossip about the events of this morning," he added, looking daggers at the stable hands, "let me remind you that I am the one charged with making sure that your wages are paid."

This veiled threat had the effect of wiping the grins from their faces, and nothing could have been more respectful than the bowed heads and tugged forelocks which accompanied Susannah's departure from the premises.

"But what am I to wear, then?" she asked as he frog-marched her in the direction of the house.

"Heavens, I don't know anything about ladies' apparel," he said, covering his own embarrassment with brusqueness. "What did you wear when you rode back in Kentucky?"

"A skirt and bodice. Not the one I wore yesterday morning—that was my good one—but another."

"Very well, then, that will suffice until a riding habit can be made for you," Peter said, although he had to wonder, if the garments he'd already seen were the best she owned, what the others must look like.

* * *

Sir Matthew Pitney, having been invited inside by a singularly unenthusiastic Miss Hawthorne, had been quick to avail himself of the invitation. Now, ensconced in the drawing room, he plied her with questions regarding the young American woman who was soon (he said) to replace her as the mistress of Ramsay Hall.

"Nonsense!" Jane protested this description. "It is impossible for her to replace me, for I never was mistress of Ramsay Hall. I was companion to the dowager Lady Ramsay, as you know, but since her death my position has been no more than a place holder."

"And no place was ever held more fetchingly, I assure you," he said with ponderous gallantry.

"You are too kind, Sir Matthew," she said in a

toneless voice meant to depress further attempts at flirtation.

"Not at all." He stepped nearer and lowered his voice conspiratorially. "It pains me, my dear, to see you in so intolerable a situation. Only say the word, and—"

He broke off abruptly as the door flew open and Lord Ramsay entered the room, clearly dressed for riding. "What brings you here so early, Sir Matthew? Nothing amiss at the Grange, I trust."

Thwarted in his object, Sir Matthew had no choice but to retreat. "Amiss? No, no, not at all. I confess, I am curious about this American cousin of yours. I'm not the sort to indulge in idle gossip, mind you, but last Sunday after church Miss Amelia said something that gave me to understand an Interesting Announcement was to be forthcoming." He cast a glance about the room as if expecting to find Susannah hiding under a chair or concealed behind the curtains. "When am I to have the pleasure of paying my respects?"

"Soon, I daresay, but not today," Richard said in a voice that brooked no argument. "She has only recently arrived, and wishes to replenish her wardrobe before being obliged to do the pretty before all the neighbors. You know how women are."

"Yes, yes, of course," agreed Sir Matthew, who in fact had no idea how women were, else he would have been less importunate in his attentions to Miss Hawthorne. He prowled restlessly about the room, pausing at length before the large window adorning the house's western façade. "Hullo, what's this? I didn't know young Peter was in the petticoat line."

Richard frowned, thinking Peter and Susannah should have been well away from the house by this time. "He isn't, so far as I know, but given that he is twenty-three years old, it should hardly be surprising if he were."

"No, indeed!" agreed the baronet, chuckling. "It appears your cousin has found himself a red-haired charmer."

Fearing the worst, Jane crossed the room to look out the window. Although concealed from the waist down by a hedge, Peter and Susannah could be seen entering the house by a side entrance in a manner which could only be described as furtive. She had no time to wonder over this curious circumstance, however, for it behooved her to silence Sir Matthew before he could further malign Susannah.

"That, Sir Matthew," she said with a sigh, "is our cousin, Miss Ramsay."

"Miss Hawthorne!" He turned from the window to stare at his inamorata. "*That* is the woman who will replace you as mistress here? But she—she—" For the first time in living memory, words apparently failed him.

"May I remind you, sir, that you are speaking of the future Lady Ramsay," said Richard at his most aristocratic.

"As I have said before, Sir Matthew, Miss Ramsay is not 'replacing' me," Jane insisted.

"No, for I am depending on my cousin Jane to instruct Miss Ramsay in everything she needs to know," Richard continued. "Surely you must agree there is no one better qualified to do so. Indeed, both Miss Ramsay and I should be quite lost without her."

"Oh, quite so, quite so!" blustered Sir Matthew, and under different circumstances, Jane might have been amused by his clumsy efforts at covering his error. "Still, my lord, she seems an odd sort of female for you to marry. I should have thought you more fastidious in your tastes."

"Do not let her current appearance deceive you," Richard cautioned. "Miss Ramsay's birth is as respectable as your own, and she is a considerable heiress besides."

"Indeed, yes!" Jane agreed. "Furthermore, Madame Lavert predicts that once she is properly gowned and coiffed, Miss Ramsay will take Society by storm as an Original."

"You intend to present her at Court, then?"

"Surely it would be very odd if Lady Ramsay were *not* presented at Court," Richard pointed out. "I daresay Society will take her to its collective bosom as an exotic. And so she is. Why, she introduced Antoine to her native cuisine only last night, and the fellow was quite beside himself."

Jane choked and turned toward the window in order to hide the laughter she could not quite suppress.

"Antoine?" echoed Sir Matthew, clearly impressed. "That Frenchie chef of yours?"

"None other." Heedless of his cousin's shaking shoulders, he told her, "Cousin Jane, we must have Sir Matthew join us one evening for dinner, so that we may introduce him to the local cuisine of Kentucky. Sir Matthew, I believe I can say without exaggeration that it will be like nothing you have ever tasted."

"Wicked man!" she scolded him some quarter of an hour later when Sir Matthew finally took his leave, having failed in his primary object of seizing an opportunity to press his suit. "If we find ourselves being obliged to host Sir Matthew to dinner, you will have no one but yourself to blame!"

"It would be almost worth it, to see Sir Matthew eat squirrel. Should we tell him what it is beforehand, or wait until his mouth is full?"

"Oh, wait, by all means!"

"I do have to wonder, though, how Antoine contrived to acquire squirrels on such short notice when it is not hunting season."

Jane smiled. "I think it is probably best not to inquire." Her amusement faded, and she continued in a more serious vein. "I am sorry you missed your opportunity to go riding with Susannah. I am not quite certain why you felt compelled to cancel your plans, but I was grateful for your assistance in fending off Sir Matthew's impertinent questions."

Richard made a noncommittal noise, but offered no explanation for his actions. There were, as she had said, some things which it was better not to question too closely.

9

Too poor for a bribe, and too proud to importune,
He had not the method of making a fortune.
THOMAS GRAY, *On His Own Character*

*B*y taking the back stairs, Susannah contrived to reach her room unobserved and, after changing her clothes, soon returned, adequately if inelegantly dressed for riding. They retraced their steps back to the stable, where Peter introduced his cousin to the docile mare named Daffodil.

"Aren't you a pretty girl," cooed Susannah, stroking the horse's nose and proffering the apple she'd pilfered from the breakfast room for that very purpose.

"Hardly a girl," Peter said. "Old Daffy must be twenty if she is a day."

Cupping a hand to the side of her mouth, Susannah leaned forward to address the horse in a stage whisper. "Pay him no heed, Daffodil, for he has no manners at all. Even in America, we know better than to make disparaging remarks about a lady's age."

Daffodil chose this moment to toss her head as if in agreement with this assessment of Peter's character, sending both Peter and Susannah, as well as the nearby stable hands, into gales of laughter.

"I beg your pardon, Miss Daffodil," Peter said meekly. To Susannah, he added, "I believe Jane used to ride her when she first came to live here, but now she prefers Andromeda, so Daffy here will be glad of the exercise. If you have any difficulty with her, though, I'm sure Lord Ramsay would be willing to purchase a more suitable mount for you."

"The female who can't handle Daffy hadn't ought to be riding at all," grumbled the groom as he placed Jane's sidesaddle on the mare's back and tightened the girth.

Peter silenced him with a frown. "Yes, well, we can't know until Miss Ramsay tries her paces, can we?"

While the groom held the horse, Peter made a stirrup of his hands and tossed his cousin into the saddle, then mounted Sheba while Susannah arranged her skirts and the groom adjusted the stirrup for Miss Ramsay's shorter stature.

When she was ready, the pair set out. Peter, uncertain of his cousin's skill in the saddle, fell back and allowed her to precede him in order to observe her before deciding on a route for them to take.

He was pleasantly surprised. The rather gauche and uncertain Susannah of the drawing room had vanished, and she sat erect and confident in the saddle, her spine straight and her shoulders back.

"I thought we might explore the eastern boundaries of the estate this morning," he said, hastily revising his idea of limiting their explorations to the smoothest and most well-travelled tracks. "There is a stream with a small waterfall which is held to be quite picturesque."

Susannah readily agreed to this plan, and they turned the horses' heads to the east. Further surprises were in store for Peter, however, for when they reached the downs beyond the Home Wood, Susannah tossed a mischievous smile over her shoulder at him.

"Shall we spring 'em?"

Without waiting for a response, she urged her mount into a gallop. Daffodil, rarely allowed such an opportunity, was nothing loth, and soon horse and rider were both flying over the broad green expanse of meadow. Peter, watching in some consternation, discovered that either his cousin was a born horsewoman, or she had been very well taught—or both. Indeed, the girl and her mount seemed to move as a single entity—and there was no question as to which was controlling it. Sheba needed no coaxing to follow, and as Peter pursued his cousin, he felt rather as if he had been played for a fool.

But no, Susannah had never claimed to be an inexperienced rider, and he had never bothered to ask. If anyone was at fault for the misunderstanding, it was he, for making erroneous assumptions.

She had stopped at the top of the rise to allow him to catch up, and when he reached her he noted that her cheeks had acquired a rosy glow, her eyes were sparkling, and her hair was coming down—again.

"My dear cousin, who taught you to ride?" he demanded, tamping down a feeling of ill-usage which he acknowledged to be groundless.

"My father," she said with more than a hint of pride. And why not? Peter thought ruefully. No doubt she was pleased to have earned the unqualified approval of a member of her family for the first time since arriving in England.

"Your father," he murmured. "Of course."

And her father would no doubt have been taught by *his* father, who had been a British cavalry officer. However he might have neglected his daughter's upbringing in other ways, Mr. Gerald Ramsay had not stinted on her equestrian education. Peter, mentally contrasting her elegant posture with her dowdy costume, resolved to speak to Richard about purchasing her an animal worthy of her skill; clearly, it was Daffodil who was not up to Susannah's weight, rather than the other way 'round. He tried to picture Richard's reaction upon seeing his bride on horseback, properly mounted and outfitted in a stylish riding habit. Suddenly conscious of a hollow feeling in the pit of his stomach, he shook off the unfamiliar sensation and addressed his cousin.

"The stream I spoke of is just over the next ridge." He pointed to a spot in the middle distance. "If poor Daffodil has the energy left after her exertions, we'll go, shall we?"

She leaned forward to pat the mare's glossy neck. "Of course she has the energy! She enjoyed the exercise very much—didn't you, girl?"

Daffodil gave a snort which Peter could have sworn indicated agreement, and they set out once more at a more sedate pace.

"Oh!" Susannah exclaimed as the stream and its miniature waterfall came into view. "It looks very familiar. There is a painting of it in the drawing room, is there not?"

"As a matter of fact, yes. I believe it was done by Cousin Jane some years ago." Suddenly conscious of having neglected a simple courtesy, he added, "I say, do you paint—or sketch, perhaps? We might have brought your sketch pad or paints—"

She shook her head. "I don't know if I can paint or not, for I've never tried." Her lips twisted in a wry grimace. "You will have noticed by now that I am sadly lacking in feminine accomplishments."

"I don't know about that. No one could fault your riding, in any case. I don't believe I've ever seen a female with a better seat."

"Oh, but that isn't a feminine accomplishment—on the Kentucky frontier, the ability to ride is a necessity! And we do breed horses, you know—Papa and I, that is—so there was never any question of my acquiring the skill."

"You say you breed horses? What kind?"

"Tennessee walkers, mostly. We usually have about forty at any given time. And, of course, sufficient pasture for grazing in summer and fodder in winter."

"Slave labour?" Peter asked.

"Not any longer, for Papa freed them in his will. Most stayed on, although a few went north to Ohio." Peter's tone had been carefully neutral, but Susannah must have sensed his disapproval, for she added quickly, "They were well treated, I assure you. Papa had the utmost contempt for people who mistreated their slaves. In fact, he and Mr. Samuels—our nearest neighbor, you know—had quite a falling-out over it. There had been some talk of a match between me and Mr. Samuels's oldest son, but Papa said any man who would mistreat his slaves would very likely treat his women and children no better, and would not allow Jonathan Samuels to come courting."

"I am pleased to know that your father was so conscientious," Peter said, choosing his words with care, "but surely the absence of cruelty, even the presence of kindness, is a poor substitute for the freedom to determine one's own fate."

In all her eighteen years, it had never occurred to Susannah that kind old Uncle Nate or Aunt Hepzibah might want something more from life than to serve as occasional playmate and surrogate parent to a motherless little girl. The realization put her on the defensive, and she spoke more harshly to Peter than she otherwise might have done. "It seems to me that you have no room to talk! As I understand it, slaves in the American South have a much lighter burden than those on the sugar plantations of the British West Indies."

He threw up his hands in mock surrender. "If you are looking for a quarrel, Cousin, you will not get it from me. I deplore the practice of slavery in my own country every bit as much as I do in yours."

"And—and Richard?"

"He shares my sentiments. In fact, he has spoken on the subject in the Lords. Parliament," he explained, seeing her puzzled expression. "Much like your own Congress, I believe, although probably a great deal stuffier."

She smiled at that, and they were once more on the friendliest of terms. They had reached the stream by this time, and agreed to walk along its banks while the horses refreshed themselves. Peter dismounted, and then turned to assist his cousin.

"Such courtly manners!" exclaimed Susannah, who on her Kentucky homestead had been obliged to fend for herself. "I feel like a princess from a fairy tale."

She lifted her knee over the pommel, kicked her foot free of the stirrup, and slid out of the saddle and into his arms. Peter was not tall, but neither was Susannah, and she was obliged to look up at him to thank him for this courtesy. Their eyes met and held, and although she opened her mouth, the words she had intended to say somehow stuck in her throat.

Peter, suddenly conscious of the feel of her trim waist beneath his hands, abruptly dropped his arms and took a stumbling step backwards.

"I'd best see to the horses," he said, and suited the word to the deed. He took the reins of both horses and led them to the stream, looping the reins over the low branches of a willow overhanging the water. While the horses drank greedily, Peter turned back to Susannah and offered his arm. "Shall we?"

They strolled along the bank for some time, while Peter plied Susannah with questions about her home in America. This, he soon learned, had very little in common with stately Ramsay Hall, consisting of only two rooms with a dogtrot running between them.

"A dogtrot?" echoed Peter, unfamiliar with the term.

"Sort of a wide corridor, open on both ends," she explained. "Since it is under the same roof as the rooms on either side, it makes a nice, shady place to sit in the summertime—much better than a porch, really, for it catches every breeze."

"I see. And the two rooms?"

"One is the bedroom, and the other is the kitchen. It also serves as what I suppose you might call a drawing room, but Papa and I never had much time for sitting and drinking tea."

"My dear cousin!" Peter hardly knew whether to be intrigued or appalled at the thought of so primitive an existence. "Life at Ramsay Hall must seem like the stuff of fairy tales."

Susannah's brow puckered as she considered this observation. "In some ways, yes, I suppose it does.

Although it never before occurred to me how very uncomfortable it must have been for Cinderella. How did she ever learn to dance at that ball anyway, when her stepmother made her work all the time?"

"Very true! I confess, I never thought of that. Perhaps the glass slippers did the dancing for her."

She shook her head. "No, for surely the fairy godmother must have mentioned it, if that had been the case."

"Well then, I suppose her father must have engaged a dancing master for her at some time before his death—a very wise investment, obviously."

She snatched her hand from his arm and stepped back. "You are saying it was very *un*wise of Papa not to do so for me!"

"I said no such thing!" Peter protested hastily, although privately his thoughts had been running along very similar lines. It was obvious to the meanest intelligence that Mr. Gerald Ramsay had been shockingly neglectful of his daughter's upbringing— except where her skill on horseback was concerned and this, by her own admission, was more out of necessity than any desire to render her a suitable bride for a gentleman of property. Peter found himself wondering what might have become of her had not Richard decided to offer for her.

"Papa was not always so—so hermitlike," Susannah said, apparently feeling some defense of her father was called for. "He and Mama used to spend part of every year in Richmond—Mama was quite the Virginia belle, if her portrait does not lie—but after she died, he closed up the town house and took me to Kentucky. We have lived there ever since. The town house was pointed out to me when I went to Richmond to visit Papa's solicitor, but I haven't been inside it since I was two years old, so I don't remember anything about it. It is tall and narrow, with a red brick façade and white columns on the portico, and black shutters on all the windows."

"It sounds very handsome," Peter said, and was surprised to discover that he meant it.

"Oh, it is, at least from the outside. But it has been closed up for more than fifteen years, so I daresay the inside needs a good airing, and very possibly more."

"If it has been standing vacant all this time, I should think it very likely. It appears Richard may need to engage an agent to oversee the American property."

The mention of her fiancé was sufficient to erase the animation from her face. "There is to be a ball to announce the betrothal, you know," she said, her voice expressionless.

"Ah," Peter said cryptically, understanding the

reason for her sudden concern as to how Cinderella acquired her dancing skills.

"Cousin Jane says she will teach me to dance—she and Aunt Amelia and Cousin Richard."

"If she says she will teach you, then you may count on her to do so," he assured her. "Depend upon it, she will not throw you to the wolves all unprepared. And as she is a very graceful dancer herself, you may be sure you are in good hands as far as your instructress is concerned."

She raised wide, troubled eyes to his. "Yes, but—but what if I'm not—what if I can't—"

He took both of her hands in his and gave them a comforting little squeeze. "If I can learn to dance, anyone can. Like you, I had not the advantage of a dancing master either. It was not until after I came here to work for Richard that the Aunts informed me I might be expected to fill in socially on occasions when an extra male was needed, and that it was my duty as a Ramsay not to disgrace myself or my name—and to tell you the truth, I suspect it was the latter that weighed most heavily with them. Between the pair of them, they took me in hand—along with assistance from Cousin Jane and Richard—and today I can at least contrive to get through a quadrille or a cotillion without treading on a lady's toes."

"I suppose it's different for men," protested Susannah, unconvinced.

"Yes, for we are expected to lead," he pointed out. "Uncomfortable though it may be, your position is more to be envied than mine was." Of course, there was the small matter that she, as Lord Ramsay's affianced bride, would be the cynosure of all eyes, while he would be merely an extra male whose duty it was to see that the less desirable of the young ladies were not allowed to languish against the wall. He hoped this circumstance would not occur to her, at least not until she had achieved some degree of proficiency in the dance.

"Then you truly don't think I will have any difficulty in learning?" she asked, her expressive blue eyes pleading for confirmation.

"Truly, Cousin Susannah, I don't. Anyone who can handle a four-legged creature as well as you handled Daffodil should have no trouble at all with only your own two to manage."

She gave him an uncertain little smile, and he was gratified to know that, even if he had not been able to convince her entirely, at least he had relieved the worst of her fears.

"Will you help with the dancing lessons, Peter?" Receiving no answer, she was obliged to prompt him.

"Peter?"

They had followed the stream as it traced a wide arc around the foot of the hill. Upon rounding the curve, Peter's steps had slowed and finally ceased altogether, and he stood staring off into the distance at a mossy, slate-tiled roof rising over the treetops.

"Peter?" she said again. "What is it?"

"Fairacres," he said, pointing toward the distant roof. "The estate borders Richard's, and the house dates to the sixteenth century. You should see it from the front: mullioned windows with diamond-shaped panes, exposed timbers on the upper floors, and a great front door so wide that four men could pass through it walking abreast. They say that Queen Elizabeth once visited, and that the first Lord Ramsay was ennobled for allowing the queen and her retinue to hunt in his woods, after the royal party had denuded the Fairacres park of deer. And it is true that the barony dates back to that time, so there may be some truth to the story."

Susannah stood on tiptoe for a better look, but could see nothing but the roof cresting the tops of the trees. "Who lives there?"

Peter sighed. "No one, now. I'd like to buy the place someday and restore the house before it falls down. It would be an expensive undertaking, but the land is fertile enough that I think it could bear the cost—so long as the estate was not obliged to entertain any more royal guests," he added with a grin.

"You aren't happy working for Cousin Richard?"

"I have no complaints about Richard as an employer—far from it, in fact, for he is more than generous. But I would like to have a place of my own someday. I have ideas I should like to try, ideas about farming and animal husbandry."

"And you don't think Richard would allow it?"

He shook his head. "On the contrary, I am almost certain he would. Therein lies the problem. If I should be wrong, if my plans should fail—" He shrugged. "I should prefer to risk my own money, rather than Richard's."

"Then I think you should buy Fairacres," she pronounced with a decisive nod.

"Oh, so do I. There is only one little problem."

"What is that?"

He gave a bitter laugh. "I haven't the money. Richard pays me well, so far as stewards go, but not *that* well. My needs are small, though, so I set aside what I can out of each quarter's pay." He sighed. "At my current rate of savings, I ought to have enough put back in, oh, another thirty years."

"But that is dreadful!" she exclaimed in ready sympathy. "Is there nothing else you can do?"

"I suppose I might marry an heiress, but even assuming a likely female should wander into rural Hampshire, it is doubtful she would be interested in a potential husband with nothing to recommend him but an old County name and a distant connection to the current baron."

"Nonsense!" Susannah's bosom swelled in indignation. "*I* am an heiress, and not only have I wandered into Hampshire but I also think you would make a very nice husband."

So touched was Peter by her emphatic defense of his prospects that he ignored her garbled syntax. "I am flattered beyond words by your high opinion of me, Cousin Susannah, but since you are already promised to Richard, I can only hope to find an unattached heiress who shares it. And now, if you are ready, I think we should turn back before Sheba and Daffodil give us up for lost."

* * *

"She *what?*" demanded Richard several hours later, when the story of Susannah's adventures had been recounted to him by Jane, who had had the story from Peter.

"Really, Richard, she is the most unusual girl!" exclaimed Jane, choking back a laugh. "You must admit, she is nothing if not resourceful."

"I must admit nothing of the sort!" he growled, pacing the Aubusson carpet adorning the drawing room floor. "When I consider that your kindness to her is rewarded so shabbily—"

"Nonsense! I daresay it is my own fault, for neglecting to explain to her that a lady's riding garments are not made by a dressmaker, but by a tailor. In hindsight, I quite see that she could not have been expected to know such a thing."

"Why not?" challenged Richard. "*You* did."

"Only because your mother took it upon herself to provide for me, and was kind enough not to make a great to-do about my deficiencies, which I can assure you were many." Seeing by the slowing of his steps that he was beginning to weaken, she added, "It is not as if the dress is ruined, you know. The fabric is not torn at all, only the stitching ripped out. It can be repaired, and no one will ever be the wiser."

"*I* will," he grumbled. "Besides, that dress looked better on you."

"Yes, well, you must remember that it was made for me," she pointed out, willing herself not to set too much store by this very flattering remark which was in fact no compliment at all, but a simple statement of opinion. "Come, Richard, it is *my* dress, after all, and if *I* can see the humour in the situation, surely there is no need for *you* to take offense."

He sighed. "I suppose you are right, and I will not mention the matter to her, if that is what you wish. It is only that she has so much, and you have so little."

"*Little?*" she echoed incredulously. "Little, I? My dear Richard, surely you jest! Why, I have an entire wardrobe of lovely gowns; surely I cannot begrudge her one, whatever she may choose to do to it. Besides that, I have a very comfortable home, and a family who cares for me, and—oh, a hundred other things beside. I would not trade places with Susannah for anything!"

"Yes, I know," Richard acknowledged with a rueful smile. "Your opinion on the subject, as I recall, was quite emphatically stated."

They had not spoken of his rejected offer of marriage from that day to this, and Jane, to her chagrin, felt her cheeks burning as if that most awkward of events had taken place only the day before, instead of almost a decade earlier. Her fingers worked in agitation, pleating the folds of her muslin skirts, but she forced herself to meet his gaze, and to smile.

"You should be very thankful that I answered you as I did, else you would not have been free to offer for Susannah."

"No," he said, his expression curiously unreadable. "No, I wouldn't have, would I?"

10

Every savage can dance.
JANE AUSTEN, *Pride and Prejudice*

The following afternoon had been set aside for Susannah's first instructions in dancing. Aunt Amelia was appointed to play the pianoforte, thus freeing Jane to demonstrate the steps Susannah was to imitate. As soon as the Aunts arrived from the dower house, they and the four "young people," as Amelia and Charlotte dubbed their junior relations (including the thirty-one-year-old head of the family), repaired to the music room. While Aunt Amelia took her place at the instrument and Aunt Charlotte settled herself in a chair along the wall to observe the proceedings, the dancers paired themselves off. Susannah was partnered with Lord Ramsay, since everyone present at the ball would expect to see the betrothed pair lead out the dancing. This left Jane with

Peter, to whom she had given very similar lessons only two years earlier.

They began with the minuet. Although quite outmoded in London, and performed nowadays only in places where the elderly were wont to congregate, such as Bath or Tunbridge Wells, this antiquated dance possessed the advantage of being easy to learn and, consequently, of giving Jane the opportunity to assess her pupil's skills before moving on to the more fashionable—and complicated—cotillion, quadrille, and, of course, the waltz.

For her part, Susannah found that after the initial awkwardness, she enjoyed the lessons very much. Although she hadn't the advantage of the musical training that was—or at least should have been—part of every gently bred lady's education, she possessed an innate sense of rhythm, and her proficiency in the saddle had imbued her with a natural grace and fluidity of movement.

From the minuet, they progressed to the Sir Roger de Coverley, and Jane noted with considerable frustration that the lively and popular reel could not be done correctly with only two couples.

"Perhaps we could hold an informal little morning dance a week before the ball," she suggested. "I believe the vicar's eldest daughter is to go to London next spring for her aunt to bring her out in Society; I daresay she would welcome the opportunity to practice, and other young people in the neighborhood would very likely do so as well."

As daunting as Susannah found the prospect of displaying her newly acquired skills before a roomful of strangers her own age, she found the prospect of doing so at a formal ball in front of a glittering assembly of aristocratic strangers infinitely worse. She agreed somewhat tentatively to this program for her education, and the lessons resumed. At the end of an hour of instruction, they had covered the steps for the minuet, the Sir Roger de Coverley, the cotillion, and the quadrille (these last two with an entirely imaginary third and fourth couple, which strengthened Jane's conviction that an informal dance before the betrothal ball was necessary, if Susannah were to comport herself with confidence). Jane then exchanged a word with Aunt Amelia and, while that lady rifled through her music, announced her intention of instructing Susannah in the waltz.

For all her ignorance, Susannah was familiar with this shocking German dance, as her missionary escort aboard the *Concordia* had been quite vocal on the subject. "Are you sure I should, Cousin Jane?" she asked, rather taken aback by her elegant English cousin's determination to set her feet on the path of iniquity. "I thought—that is, I was given to understand that the waltz is not at all the thing."

"Oh, that was the case years ago, but now it is danced everywhere," Jane assured her. "Indeed, it would be thought very odd if we did not include at least one waltz, and very probably more. But pray learn the steps first, and then you may decide for yourself. It is quite simple, you know. You have only to count to three."

Jane turned to her partner to demonstrate, and Susannah, suppressing her misgivings, allowed Richard to place his right hand at her waist and take her right hand in his left. With some hesitation, she followed Jane's example and put her free hand upon her partner's shoulder, an act which brought them into such close contact that, if she crossed her eyes, she might study in minute detail the starched folds of his cravat.

Having grown up in the midst of a thriving horse-breeding enterprise, Susannah was familiar enough with the habits of animals to have a general idea of the conjugal act between men and women. It stood to reason, then, that this approximation of an embrace in the arms of the very man with whom she would soon be engaging in so intimate an act should set her senses all a-twitter, but instead she felt . . . nothing. This discovery should have been a relief, but in fact, Susannah found it vaguely disappointing. Her future husband's hand gripping hers was simply a hand; his other hand at her waist was no more than a slight pressure felt through the boned fabric of her stays.

She could not understand it; one glance at Peter and Jane in a similar hold was enough to inform her that it should have been a gross impertinence. Indeed, the sight of Peter's arm about Jane's waist was so unsettling that she lost her step, causing Richard to bump into her.

"No, no," Jane said, stepping out of Peter's hold. "You must relax, Susannah, and allow Richard to lead you. Here, Richard, let us show her. Aunt Amelia, will you begin again from the fifth measure?"

The elderly lady nodded. "Of course, Jane dear. Richard, are you ready? *One*, two, three, *one*, two, three—"

As Aunt Amelia's fingers came down on the keys, Richard took Jane in his arms and steered her in time to the music, the pair of them turning in a clockwise direction as they glided about the room.

"Oh!" Susannah breathed. "Why, it isn't wicked at all, is it? How very elegant they look!"

Peter, standing beside her, agreed. "They are very well matched, are they not?"

"They are. In fact," she added, as a new thought occurred to her, "I wonder why Richard has not married Jane."

"I confess, I have wondered that myself. They are so very compatible that I should have thought they would be well suited. But there has never been anything like that between them, so far as I know." He shrugged. "Perhaps they see no reason to spoil a perfectly good friendship with wedding vows."

"But why must one choose? Can husbands and wives not be friends as well?"

Peter shook his head. "I fear you are asking the wrong person. While I flatter myself that I have many friends, I have never had a wife, and so can offer no opinion on the subject."

As the demonstration came to an end, Susannah hoped she might be given a chance to try the waltz with Peter as her partner. It was very odd, but she felt much more comfortable with him than she did with the man who was soon to be her husband; she supposed it was because Peter was a mere "mister," just like men in America, instead of a lord. But no, as the final chord faded, Richard bowed very formally and Jane curtsied in like manner, and then both of them returned to their original partners. Stifling a pang of disappointment, Susannah allowed Richard to take her in the now familiar hold, and if she failed to match Jane's elegance of movement, at least she contrived to get through the dance without stumbling.

With this performance, the dancing lesson was concluded, and Richard let his hand fall from her waist. "If you are not exhausted from your terpsichorean efforts, Susannah, I should be pleased to show you about the portrait gallery and introduce you to your ancestors."

"Exhausted? By *dancing*?" exclaimed Susannah, who on her Kentucky homestead was accustomed to doing more physical labour by noon than her English cousins, so far as she could tell, did in a week. "Why, no, I'm not tired at all, and I would be very pleased to see my ancestors in the portrait gallery."

This proved to be a long passage lined with tall windows on one wall, presumably placed there for the purpose of illuminating the framed portraits on the other. Susannah, rather intimidated by the rows of ruffed, powdered, or bewigged Ramsays glaring down at her from their frames, paused before the likeness of a lady with wide, panniered skirts of deep blue satin balanced by a towering powdered wig adorned with a stuffed bird perched on the edge of a nest containing a trio of open-mouthed hatchlings. The stiff formality of the lady's pose was belied by the twinkle in her eye, as if she were fully aware of the absurdity of fashion, and invited the viewer to share in the joke.

"Who is she?" Susannah asked, liking the lady already.

"My mother," Richard said with a hint of pride in his voice. "She was held to be a great beauty—said to rival the famous Gunning sisters, in fact—and might have looked a great deal higher than a mere baron, had she not fallen in love with my father."

"What a romantic story!"

"I suppose it was, in some ways."

A shadow crossed his face, but Susannah, absorbed in her study of the portrait, did not notice. "She looks as if she must have been a very *happy* sort of person."

"She was—and a very kind one, as well."

"I'm sorry I never had a chance to know her."

"So am I. She would have liked you very much." Even as he said the words, he realized they were true. His mother had liked everyone, had even seen the humour in Sir Matthew Pitney's pompousness. It suddenly occurred to him that the Dowager Lady Ramsay would have laughed aloud at the tale of Susannah and her "riding costume," much as Jane had done. Resolving to be kinder to his betrothed in the future, he took Susannah's elbow and led her further along the passage.

"But is there no picture of your father?"

"On the contrary. There is a portrait by Reynolds which is said to be very fine—and indeed, it is a very accurate likeness—but it no longer hangs in the portrait gallery. When my father died, it was moved to his bedroom—which became mine, along with the title."

This mention of sleeping arrangements reminded him of an aspect of his approaching nuptials which had not yet been addressed. "I must not forget to show you my mother's bedchamber. Her tastes tended toward the rococo which was fashionable in her younger days, but you may have it redecorated according to your own preferences."

This discussion of mutual (and, presumably, adjoining) bedchambers was much too intimate for Susannah's liking. "You must have loved your father very much, to keep his picture in your bedroom," she observed, returning the conversation to the less unnerving subject of his parentage.

"Love?" Richard frowned as he pondered the matter. "I was devoted to him, of course, as a son should be, but he was too distant a parent to inspire true affection in his children. No, his portrait was placed there by my uncle, his younger brother, as a reminder to me of my obligation to my father, and to all the Lords Ramsay who preceded him."

"Oh," said Susannah, rather daunted by this revelation. "But if he loved your mother—"

"I said she fell in love with him; I never said he felt the same about her. Oh, he was never unkind to her, and certainly not cruel," he added hastily, seeing shocked dismay writ large upon her expressive countenance. "But I suspect his choice of her as a bride was inspired not so much by the tender passion as it was by my mother's genteel birth and sizeable dowry—not to mention the satisfaction of snatching the Season's reigning beauty from under the very noses of gentlemen whose social status was far superior to his."

"Your poor mama!"

"She would be very shocked by your pity, I assure you, for as you yourself noted, she was by nature a happy person. If she was at times neglected by her husband, she compensated by lavishing affection on her children and, later, on her companion, Jane Hawthorne."

"Children?" echoed Susannah, noting his use of the plural. "You have siblings, then?"

"Had," he corrected her, thinking of the family vault where three tiny bodies lay entombed, none of them having survived beyond their fifth year. Shaking off a sudden sense of melancholy, he took her elbow and led her further down the gallery. "Now that I am to be married myself, I wish Mama were still alive so that I might question her about her marriage. It might have helped me to be a better husband to you. I will do my best, but I fear I did not have the most shining of examples."

He stopped before a large painting of a young man astride a prancing black steed. The rider's curled and powdered wig dated the portrait to the previous century, and his scarlet coat identified him as an officer in His Majesty's army. "Now, here is a portrait that might interest you."

" 'Captain Benjamin Ramsay,' " she read aloud from the small brass nameplate at the bottom of the frame, then looked up at Richard, wide-eyed. "But that would make him—"

"Your grandfather," he said, nodding. "I gather this is the first time you've ever seen his likeness?"

"Yes, for he died before I was born." She leaned closer, peering intently at the painted face. "I don't look much like him, do I?"

"No." Richard saw no point in denying the obvious. "I daresay you resemble your mother, or perhaps your grandmother."

But Susannah had already moved on to the next painting, a man with dark eyes and black King Charles curls hanging down to his shoulders. One hand rested on the hilt of his sword, and the other stroked the head of a sleek greyhound.

"A very dashing cavalier, don't you think?" Richard asked. "He was the fourth Baron Ramsay, but I have always thought that if we could cut his hair and shave his moustache, he would look just like Peter."

Susannah, determined to put this theory to the test, closed one eye and raised her finger to hide the pencil-thin moustache, then giggled at the result. "You're right—he does! What a pity this betrothal ball can't be a masquerade. Peter's costume would be quite settled!" Her smile faded as she recalled the discussion she'd had with him the previous day during their ride. "Richard, what do you intend to do about Peter?"

He frowned. " 'Do?' I wasn't aware that I had to 'do' anything about him. What are you thinking?"

"Surely he can't wish to remain your steward forever," she pointed out.

"Why the dev—why the deuce shouldn't he?" demanded Richard, taken aback by this hitherto unconsidered possibility. "He is well paid and, being a member of the family, he has a degree of freedom he would be unlikely to find in anyone else's employ."

"I didn't mean to suggest that he might seek a position elsewhere," she objected. "But he is young and ambitious, and—and sooner or later, he will want a broader scope for his talents."

He regarded her in utter bewilderment. "What do you know of his ambitions, let alone his talents? Why, you've hardly known him a se'ennight!"

Susannah, realizing by now that she was the recipient of confidences to which Richard had not been privy, hastily demurred. "No, but—well, he seems to be very intelligent, and—"

"Oh, he is," Richard readily concurred. "That is why I should hate to lose him."

"But he wants—that is, he may wish to be the master of his own establishment someday," she persisted. "I thought perhaps you might, I don't know, settle something on him that would allow him to marry well."

Richard's eyebrows all but disappeared into his hairline. "Give him a *dowry*, you mean, like a bride? My dear girl, he would be insulted at the very suggestion!"

"Yes," she said, acknowledging the truth of this assertion with a sigh. "Yes, I suppose he would, wouldn't he?"

"But enough about Peter. Tell me, what do you think of this painting? I think you may find its subject strangely familiar."

He steered her toward a sixteenth-century likeness,

somewhat faded with age, of a young woman whose long, slender neck rose with elegant grace from the stiff folds of her wide ruff. Her hair was dark, but the serene smile, straight nose, and the twinkle in the grey eyes were instantly recognizable.

"Oh!" Susannah exclaimed, allowing herself to be distracted from the delicate subject of Peter's future. "She looks just like Cousin Jane!"

"I have always thought so."

Richard's expression softened as he regarded the familiar features, and Susannah, seeing this unconscious reaction, was emboldened to voice the question that had puzzled her since she'd watched her cousins waltzing together.

"Cousin Richard, I was just wondering—"

"Yes?" prompted when she broke off. "What is it?"

"You may think it impertinent of me to ask," she cautioned him, reluctant to commit another such *faux pas* as she had obviously made concerning Peter.

"Nonsense! You may ask me anything you like, and I will do my best to give you an answer."

"Very well, then. When I saw you and Cousin Jane waltzing, it occurred to me to wonder why the two of you have never married."

He stiffened and might have given her a stinging set-down, had he not just assured her of his willingness to answer any question she might care to ask. And in this case, it was perhaps best to make a clean breast of the matter, lest she hear of it from some other source and ascribe his silence to some entirely erroneous cause. Yes, it was better to make a full confession and put the issue to rest; it was, after all, ancient history.

"As a matter of fact, I made her an offer of marriage almost ten years ago, which she very politely declined."

"Really?" Wide blue eyes regarded him curiously.

"Her father had just died, and she was left virtually penniless. I considered it my duty to offer her the protection of my name."

Susannah sniffed in disdain. "If you said *that* to her, I don't wonder she turned you down!"

"I said something very similar in my letter to you, and you accepted me!" he retorted, goaded into discourtesy.

"Yes, but—but that was different." Her gaze shifted away from his, to drift down the passage toward the fourth Baron Ramsay.

"How so?"

"I had been left all alone, much like Cousin Jane, but far from being penniless, I was heiress to a con-siderable fortune, according to Papa's lawyer. He urged me to marry as quickly as possible, but all the candidates for my hand—not that there were all that many of them, for we didn't get out much—were far more interested in my inheritance than they were in me. Then your letter came, and I figured that even if you turned out to be perfectly beastly, at least you wouldn't be marrying me only for my fortune. And sure enough, you turned out to be not beastly at all—well, except for that first night, and I've quite forgiven you for that."

"My dear Susannah, such praise! You unman me!"

She giggled. "Well, you did ask!"

"So I did." He took her arm and led her further down the gallery, echoing with a sigh, "So I did."

11

These violent delights have violent ends.
WILLIAM SHAKESPEARE, *Romeo and Juliet*

The following morning, Susannah sat alone in the drawing room, taking advantage of the light streaming through its tall east-facing windows to illuminate her work as she effected repairs to her borrowed gown. She was halfway finished with the last of the two long side seams, and had just inserted the needle into the fabric for the next stitch when the sound of a gentleman clearing his throat startled her, and she jabbed the point into her thumb. Pressing the offended digit to her mouth, she looked up and saw Richard hovering in the doorway, looking more like an unwelcome visitor than the lord of the manor.

"Susannah, have you a moment? I should like to speak to you, if I may."

His obvious discomfort communicated itself to her, and the fingers of her uninjured hand closed on the pile

155

of figured muslin in her lap. "Of course, Richard."

"Yes, well." He crossed the room with measured steps, and seated himself on the edge of the wing chair facing hers. "I think it is time we set a date for this marriage. I thought perhaps three weeks from Thursday, if that is agreeable to you."

"So—so soon?" Her hands jerked convulsively, and the borrowed gown slid from her lap to pool in a heap at her feet.

"Can you think of any compelling reason to wait? The sooner we are wed, the sooner your rather precarious position is settled."

"There is that," she admitted, casting a furtive glance at her thumb to make sure the bleeding had stopped.

"By setting the date for three weeks hence, we should be able to hold the ball in a fortnight, and the wedding a week after. Tell me, would you prefer it to take place here at Ramsay Hall, or at the church in the village?"

"A ball in a church?" exclaimed Susannah, scandalized.

"Not the ball," Richard said with some asperity. "The wedding."

"Oh. That." She fixed her gaze on the hands in her lap. "I have no preference one way or the other."

"Well then, if it is all the same to you, I think we should marry in church."

"Very well."

"Will you want Jane to stand up with you, or would you prefer a bridesmaid nearer your own age? The vicar has two daughters who might serve the purpose, as well as a visiting niece from the West Indies who is rumored to be a considerable heiress. The two of you might find you have a lot in common."

She shook her head. "Thank you, but I think I should prefer Jane to a stranger."

"Very well. I expect Peter will attend me, so we shall be a family party." He shifted on the edge of his seat. "That only leaves the matter of the wedding trip. Should you like to spend a few weeks in Paris, or would you prefer a longer trip to Rome?"

"*Weeks?*"

He nodded. "Or months, if we sail to Italy."

So taken aback was Susannah by the proposed length of such a trip that she forgot, at least for the nonce, its primary purpose. "Surely you cannot wish to be away from your estate for so long!"

"My dear Susannah, even after the honeymoon we will not remain in the country all the year 'round. I am accustomed to spending every spring and autumn in London, while Parliament is in session. As my wife, you will of course accompany me on those occasions, so we might as well begin as we mean to go on."

"But what about the spring planting, and the autumn harvest?"

He shrugged. "Peter will see to it, as always." Seeing she was not convinced, he added, "The estate could not be in better hands, I assure you."

Of this, at least, she had no doubt. Still, it seemed wrong of Richard to burden Peter with the entire running of the estate while the two of them went gadding about on the Continent. "In that case, I should like to see Paris, if you please," she decided, although her selection owed more to the shorter duration of such a trip than to the glory of Versailles or the medieval splendour of Notre Dame.

"As you wish. I shall speak to the vicar about the arrangements for the wedding." He rose from his chair, bobbed a self-conscious little bow, and left the room.

Alone once more, Susannah stared blindly down at the gown on the drawing room floor as if wondering how it had come to be there—wondering, indeed, how *she* had come to be there. Left alone in the world after the death of her father, Richard's letter had seemed a godsend; in fact, there had been something terribly romantic about the idea of crossing the ocean to marry a wealthy and aristocratic stranger. Now that a date for the union had been set, however, her approaching marriage was no longer a vague idea. Now it was *real* in a way it had not been before.

And what did you expect? she scolded herself mentally. *It's a marriage, not a public execution. Women do it every day.*

Still, she was thankful for the sewing that demanded her attention and, eventually, was able to set the last few stitches with fingers that hardly shook at all. Having completed this task, she knotted the seam, snipped the thread, and left the room with the repaired gown draped over her arm.

"Ah, Miss Ramsay," the butler addressed her as she crossed the hall, proffering a folded paper. "A message just came for you from Madame Lavert."

She took the paper, opened it, and scanned the brief missive. "Madame says the first of my new dresses will be delivered tomorrow." She glanced at the gown hanging over her arm. "I suppose I can return this one to Jane. Will you see that it is laundered?"

"May I suggest that you keep it to wear today, and return it to Miss Hawthorne upon the morrow? If you will permit me, miss, I will take it to the laundry maid; daresay it will need ironing after its, er, adventures. "

"Yes, thank you." She surrendered the garment to the butler. "I don't *think* it has any bloodstains on it, but will you ask her to look and make sure?"

The butler raised his eyebrows but made no reply before bearing the dress away with a dignity befitting the crown jewels.

Susannah gazed regretfully at the great curving staircase. Her experience in the stables had been sufficient to inform her that the narrow-skirted gowns she would be expected to wear every day would be just as unsuited for sliding down the banister as they would be for riding. With a sigh of regret for what might have been, she looked down at the note in her hands.

It was here that Peter found her a moment later, when he emerged from his office and saw at once from her troubled expression that something was not right.

"Susannah? Is something wrong?"

"Wrong? Oh, no!" Her smile was much too bright, and too fixed, to be genuine. "A date has been set for the wedding."

He frowned at the paper in her hand. "And Richard saw fit to inform you of it in a letter? Is that the best he could do?"

"No, of course not! This is from Madame Lavert. She says some of my new clothes will be delivered tomorrow."

"I see. Forgive me, cousin, but most females of my acquaintance would be over the moon at the prospect of a whole new wardrobe, instead of looking as if they'd just lost their last friend."

"Oh, it isn't that, it's just—" She cast a longing glance at the staircase. "I suppose now I'll never slide down the banister."

"In that case, you'd best do it now, before your new finery arrives."

Her expression lightened at once, and she started for the foot of the stairs. "I suppose you're right. Let's go, then, shall we?"

Peter's eyebrows rose in alarm. "Who, me?"

"You said you'd always wanted to," she reminded him. "Besides, I won't do it without you."

He should not; he knew he should not. And yet, surely seeing the bleak look vanish from her face was worth a temporary loss of dignity. "Very well, then," he said, conceding defeat. "Lead on!"

Susannah needed no further urging. She scampered up the stairs, with Peter following close behind. When she reached the top, she turned to her co-conspirator. "Will you go first, or shall I?"

"After you," he said, indicating the polished oak banister with a sweep of one arm.

Grinning broadly, Susannah braced herself on the railing with one hand, then hitched up her skirts with the other and swung her leg over, seating herself astride the banister with her back facing the hall below. "Ready . . . set . . ."

"Go!" they said in unison, and she pushed off.

Peter, watching from the top of the stairs, was treated to the spectacle of flying hair and flapping skirts as she rounded the curve of the stairs on her descent. Her flight was finally halted by the newel post at the bottom of the stairs, and she dismounted and raised a beaming face to his.

"Oh, that was wonderful! You'll love it, Peter, I know you will!"

Ruthlessly silencing the voice in his head that argued for propriety, Peter followed Susannah's example and swung his leg over the banister—a much easier task for him than it had been for his cousin, as he was unhindered by skirts. A moment later he was sailing downward, pleasurably aware of the floor rushing up at him, the breeze created by his descent as it ruffled his hair, and the young woman beaming at him from below. He had almost reached her when a noise from above drew his attention, and he looked up to discover in some dismay his rapidly shrinking employer staring at him in horrified fascination from the top of the stairs.

"What the devil do you think you're doing?" demanded Richard, just as Peter bumped into the newel post, bringing his descent to an abrupt halt.

"Richard!" He scrambled off the banister, hastily formulating and rejecting several explanations for his uncharacteristic behavior. "I beg your pardon. We—I was just—"

"Never mind," Richard cut him off brusquely. "I'm quite aware of what you were doing. What I should like to know is why you thought it would be a good idea."

"I just thought—you see, I'd never—" Peter abandoned the hopeless task. How did one defend the indefensible? "I beg your pardon, Richard. It—it will not happen again."

"It was my fault," Susannah spoke up. "The first time I saw this room, I told Peter I should like to slide down the banister, and although he told me at the time that it would be very improper to do so, he did it to oblige me."

"It's not as if you held a gun to my head!" protested Peter, determined not to let her bear the blame for his own indiscretion. "Besides, you were—are—new here, and unfamiliar with our ways. I haven't your excuse. I knew—I should not have—"

"But I'm the one who—"

"No, I can't let you accept responsibility for my—"

"If you will have done with flagellating yourself, Peter," put in Richard, interrupting what showed every sign of being a protracted debate, "I have a task for you. I was coming to inform you of it when I discovered you at your revelries, or whatever you choose to call them."

"Yes, of course," Peter said hastily. "What is it you want me to do?"

"I shall require accommodations in Paris for myself and Susannah following the wedding. You will write to the Maison Blanche in the Rue St. Honouré and ask if they can oblige me with rooms for, say, three weeks at the end of August."

"Yes, my lord." Peter cast an apologetic glance at Susannah, then betook himself from the room.

"So I'm 'my lord,' am I?" Richard muttered. "He does have a guilty conscience, doesn't he?"

Alone with her fiancé, Susannah hung her head. "Please don't blame Peter. He didn't want to do it—that is, he confessed he'd always *wanted* to slide down the banister, but he never would have actually *done* it, had I not urged him to it." She ventured a look at him through her lashes. "Are you going to dismiss him?"

"Dismiss Peter? Good God, no! He's the best steward I ever had. No, I shall probably give him a tongue-lashing, and tell him that such carryings-on are, or ought to be, beneath the dignity of a Ramsay, and that I do not employ him to engage in the sort of hijinks which he should have outgrown a decade ago—facts of which he is no doubt already well aware—but I have no intention of cutting off my nose merely to spite my face." He bent a stern gaze upon the top of her bowed head. "I trust I shall have no reason in future to ring a similar peal over my wife."

"No, my lord," she said meekly.

"Cousin Richard," he corrected her.

She looked up at him then, the hint of a smile trembling at the corners of her mouth. "I am sorry to contradict you, but I must agree with Peter. When you take that tone, and look down your nose in such a way, you are very much 'my lord.' "

"In that case, I trust that once we are wed, you will conduct yourself in a manner befitting 'my lady,' "

Susannah tilted her head and considered the matter. "Well, I'll *try*, but I make no promises, for I don't know how 'my lady' is *supposed* to behave. I am glad you don't intend to punish Peter, though."

"My dear girl, I never said I didn't intend to punish him, only that I didn't intend to dismiss him." Seeing her puzzled expression, he explained, "Clearly, you have never been on the receiving end of one of my reprimands."

"Oh," said Susannah, rather daunted.

She started up the stairs, and Richard felt compelled to ask, "I trust you are not going up to have

165

another go at the banister?"

She paused on the third riser, then turned, lifted her chin, and looked down her nose at him. "I am going to my room to change my clothes for luncheon, which I believe is the custom here. Or do you intend to come and watch, to make sure I do that to your satisfaction?"

"No. At least," he added smoothly, "not yet."

"Oh!" Susannah, blushing furiously, turned and hurried up the stairs as if fearful he might change his mind.

Chuckling a little over his bride's hasty departure, Richard lingered in the hall puzzling over the uncharacteristic behavior of his steward when Jane entered the house, having spent an agreeable morning in the garden. Upon seeing the odd expression on his face, she took off her broad-brimmed hat and laid it aside, along with the basket of flowers she'd cut, and joined him at the foot of the stairs.

"Richard? What is the matter?"

He shook his head in bewilderment. "I've just interrupted the most bizarre scene. I came out of my room and reached the top of the stairs just in time to see Peter sliding down the banister."

"Did you?" Jane choked back a gurgle of laughter. "How—how very odd!"

"Had I been a little earlier," he continued, "I might

have observed the future Lady Ramsay similarly engaged."

"Ah, that explains it," she said, nodding sagely. "Depend upon it, Susannah was behind it. She really is the most unusual girl!"

"Oh, she admitted as much! I suppose I must pardon her behavior on the grounds of ignorance, but Peter has no such excuse, for he surely must have known better. I can't imagine why he allowed her to persuade him into betraying such a want of conduct."

She shook her head. "I doubt she could have persuaded him to do anything that he did not wish to do. Really, Richard, is it possible that you have lived here all your life, and have never once slid down the banister?"

Richard had the grace to look ashamed. "Not since I was twelve years old, anyway."

"And that was almost twenty years ago! I think you have shown a quite remarkable restraint."

"But Peter is not twelve years old," he pointed out. "Nor, for that matter, is Susannah."

"No, but I daresay she has never seen such a staircase in her life, so she has never before had the opportunity. As for Peter, well, it must have been a great trial to him, looking at this one every day for the last two years and believing it to be forbidden fruit. I suppose it only wanted a co-conspirator to tip him over the edge."

"Defend them all you like, but I know *you* would never behave with such a disregard for propriety!"

"No," she said sadly, regarding the forbidden banister with a rather wistful little smile. "No, I suppose I would not."

"Jane! You cannot mean to tell me that *you* have any desire to engage in such antics!"

"Oh, can I not? And here I thought we could always be honest with one another!"

"If you had any desire to slide down banisters, you surely could have done so as a child, in your father's house," he pointed out, determined to bring her to some sense of reason.

"No, for the staircase there did not have such a lovely curve as this one, and was broken in the middle by the half-landing, beside. Furthermore, the wood was not so smoothly polished, so that one would almost certainly have got splinters in one's, er, hands."

Richard was surprised into a shout of laughter. "I'll wager it was *not* your hands that concerned you! Very well, never let it be said that Peter and Susannah may enjoy an experience that is denied Jane Hawthorne."

He seized her hand and started up the stairs.

"Richard! I am hardly dressed for such an

exercise," she protested laughingly, fingering her straight skirts.

"No, you will have to sit aside, as if you were riding a horse."

"I will very likely fall and break my neck!"

"No you won't, for I shall go down with you, and hold you." Seeing her waver, he shot her a challenging look. "Fighting shy, Miss Hawthorne?"

"Never, Lord Ramsay," she shot back. "If you insist, why then, I await your pleasure."

"No time like the present. Besides, we had best complete the experiment before either Peter or Susannah returns—or, worse, both of them at once—or I shall never hear the end of it." When they reached the top of the stairs, he sat on the banister and lifted one leg over the rail, then patted the narrow strip of polished oak in front of him. "Madam, your chariot awaits."

She sat on the spot he had indicated, but when she leaned back against him, bunched her skirts together, and prepared to swing both legs over the banister, he was moved to protest. "You can't intend to slide down with nothing below your feet but twenty feet of air!"

"*You* can't expect me to make such a once-in-a-lifetime journey staring at my shoes the entire time," she retorted. "Besides, you assured me that I would be perfectly safe."

"Very well, then, if you insist." He pulled her tightly against him, locking his arms about her waist.

And then he pushed off. Jane felt the pleasantly warm friction of the polished wooden banister sliding away beneath her hands, and the no less pleasant—and no less warm—sensation of Richard's chest pressed against her back, and decided it was probably a good thing that they did not intend to make a habit of this particular activity.

Then, as they rounded the sweeping curve of the staircase, a door opened in the hall below, and the butler's shocked voice exclaimed, "Your lordship!"

Startled by the interruption and embarrassed at being caught out in such an indiscretion, Richard lost his hold on Jane. With a little squeak of sheer terror, she slipped from his grasp and toppled headlong over the railing.

"Good God!" He snatched at her, but his hands closed on empty air. "Jane!"

12

I fell as a dead body falls.
DANTE ALIGHIERI, *The Divine Comedy*

*R*ichard did not wait for the newel post at the bottom of the stairs to halt his descent, but jerked to a stop by gripping the banister with both hands. He scrambled over the railing with more speed than grace, then took the stairs two at a time and rounded the newel post to reach the spot where Jane lay. Wilson was there before him, but Richard pushed the butler aside and dropped to one knee before her inert form.

"Jane, are you all right? What a stupid question! Of course you're not all right," he muttered, turning to toss a command over his shoulder to the butler. "Bring some brandy, Wilson, and be quick about it. Jane, can you move? Can you sit up?"

Jane, dazed almost as much by the expression on

Richard's chalk-white countenance as she had been by the fall, put these questions to the test by gingerly flexing arms and legs in turn. "I—I think so."

He took her hand in his and, easing his other arm behind her shoulders, gently raised her to a sitting position. Meanwhile Peter, banished to his office in disgrace, now emerged from that chamber, lured from his lair by the sounds of commotion in the hall.

"Richard? What is—good heavens! Cousin Jane! What happened?"

"Well might you ask!" Richard retorted. "She fell from the banister. You see where that stunt has led!"

"I—I'm sorry—I never dreamed—"

"Never mind that now," Richard cut him off, uncomfortably aware that he was placing on Peter's shoulders blame that should be more rightly assigned to himself. "I should be obliged if you would ride for the doctor."

"Yes, of course." Peter strode quickly toward the door, losing no time in carrying out this command.

"And have him come at once!" Richard ordered his retreating back. "Tell him it is of the utmost urgency!"

As the door closed behind Peter, Jane felt compelled to protest. "Nonsense! I am sure I shall feel better directly, if only I may rest on the sofa for a bit."

"You, my girl, will do as you are told!" he said,

raising her to her feet nonetheless. "Can you walk?"

"I think so," she said again. "It is only that my ankle hurts so—*oh!*"

As if to prove her point, the ankle in question balked at bearing her weight, and she would have fallen had Richard not caught her against his chest. Ignoring her feeble protests, he swept her up in his arms and carried her bodily into the drawing room, where he laid her gently on the sofa. He turned to fetch a cushion to place beneath her rapidly swelling ankle, and saw Wilson hovering just inside the door holding a tray with a decanter of brandy and a single glass.

"Good man," Richard said, unstoppering the decanter and pouring a generous measure into the glass. He took it to the sofa where Jane lay, then raised her to a half-sitting position with one arm behind her shoulders while he raised the glass to her lips.

"Really, Richard, there is no need," she objected, attempting without much success to push the glass away.

"Nonsense! You've had a nasty shock; the brandy will do you good. Now, will you drink it yourself, or must I pour it forcibly down your throat?"

A surprisingly tender smile robbed his words of any real threat. Still, she submitted meekly to his demand, insisting only that she be allowed to hold the glass herself. Alas, her hands shook so badly that he was forced to steady the glass lest she slosh brandy all over herself. He glanced toward the door and, discovering that Wilson had withdrawn, leaving him alone with Jane, addressed her in a low voice.

"Jane, I am sorrier than I can say. I hope you can forgive me, for I will never forgive myself!"

"There is no need for these self-recriminations," she assured him, and he was relieved to note that her voice, at least, sounded somewhat steadier. "After all, it was my own idea, so I have no one else to blame."

"Still, if I had not agreed to it—"

"If you must insist on taking responsibility, Richard, you may console yourself with the knowledge that the accident has at least robbed me of any desire to repeat the experience."

But even as she said the words, she wondered if they were true. Until Wilson's untimely interruption, the sensation of flying had been very pleasant, and the feel of Richard's steadying arm about her waist and his broad chest against her back had been pleasanter still. And even after the fall, there had been that moment when she had looked up from where she lay on the floor and seen him staring down at her with such an expression on his white face that she had never thought to see on his usually stoic countenance. No, to surprise such a reaction from him, she was not at all sure that she would not run up the stairs (or hobble, as the case might be) and make the attempt all over again.

"I must get up," she insisted, attempting to sit up in spite of the feeling of faintness that threatened to overwhelm her. "I had promised to call on the vicar's wife this morning and bring her my receipt for quince preserves."

"Mrs. Cummings may wait until Sunday, when you can take it to her at church."

"No, for she particularly wished to make it this week," Jane protested.

"Very well, then, Susannah may act as your deputy."

"But Susannah hasn't even met Mrs. Cummings!"

"Peter can drive her to the vicarage and perform the introductions," Richard said in a voice that brooked no argument. "You are not moving from this spot until the doctor has had a chance to examine you, so you might as well resign yourself to remaining here."

He drew up a chair before the sofa and planted himself in it as if daring her to try to escape. She gave a little sigh of what might have been resignation or contentment; she was not quite sure which.

"Very well, Richard," she said meekly.

She had not long to wait, for Peter returned with

175

the doctor in a surprisingly short time, having had the good fortune to meet him on the road on his way back from a call.

"I'm glad you could come so quickly, Doctor," Richard said, surrendering his chair to the physician. "Miss Hawthorne, er, took a tumble on the stairs," he explained with perhaps less than perfect truth.

"The stupidest thing," Jane put in, but made no attempt to provide a more accurate description of the accident.

"Let's have a look, then."

The doctor took a seat in the chair Richard had vacated, and placed his black leather bag on the floor beside him. He took Jane's ankle in both hands, and began to massage it gently. She flinched as he hit a particularly tender spot, and Richard, seeing this involuntary reaction, placed a comforting hand on her shoulder.

"Fortunately, the ankle does not appear to be broken," declared the doctor at last, upon completing his examination. "Still, I would recommend—"

He was interrupted by the sudden appearance of Susannah, who burst into the room in a swirl of unfashionably full skirts and tangled russet curls. "Cousin Richard, I was just thinking—" She broke off abruptly, her eyes widening at the tableau that presented itself to her. "Oh! What has happened? Don't tell me that *Jane*—"

"Miss Hawthorne fell on the stairs," Richard said, fixing her with a gimlet stare that dared her to challenge this assertion at her peril. Having effectively silenced his betrothed, he turned back to the physician. "Susannah, allow me to present Dr. Calloway, who is tasked with preserving the health of the residents of Lower Nettleby. Dr. Calloway, Miss Ramsay, my young cousin from America. Now, Doctor, as to Miss Hawthorne's injury—you were saying?"

The doctor acknowledged Susannah with a nod, then turned back to Richard. "Yes, well, it appears the bones of the ankle are not broken, but the muscles are badly sprained. You will need to refrain from putting any weight on it for at least a week, and possibly longer," he added to Jane.

"Oh, but I can't!" she protested. "There is too much to do!"

"In that case, you will need to give your orders to the staff, and let his lordship, Miss Ramsay, and young Peter see that they are carried out." He gave her what seemed to her a rather condescending smile. "Who knows? By the time you are back on your feet, you may have decided you enjoy playing the domestic tyrant."

Jane rather doubted this, but a pleading look at

Richard left her in no doubt that he would make sure the physician's instructions were followed to the letter.

In this prediction she was entirely correct. No sooner had the doctor quitted the premises (having left a bottle of laudanum, in case the pain should make it difficult for Miss Hawthorne to sleep) than Richard informed Peter and Susannah that, since they were indirectly responsible for Jane's misfortune, they might make themselves useful.

"Susannah, you will be giving orders to the household staff soon enough, so you might as well begin now. You will require the housekeeper to write out the receipt for quince preserves. Peter, when that is done, you will drive Susannah to the vicarage, where she may give it to Mrs. Cummings with Miss Hawthorne's compliments. And from now on," he declared, "there will be no more sliding down banisters—by anyone! Is that understood?"

After Peter and Susannah had gone (having given their word in much the same manner as a pair of miscreant schoolchildren called on the carpet), Jane looked up from the sofa to regard Richard with a quizzical eye. "If your children are to have anything at all of their mother's spirit—to say nothing of your own self-professed adventures as a boy—I wish you joy in attempting to enforce such a prohibition."

"Yes," he agreed in a flat voice. "Joy, indeed."

* * *

Meanwhile Peter and Susannah, having obtained the promised receipt from the housekeeper, betook themselves to the stables, where Peter instructed the groom to hitch his lordship's big bay to the gig. Ever since the groom had learned of Susannah's skill in the saddle, there had been nothing but the utmost respect in his demeanor toward his future mistress. In fact, she was obliged to listen in silent and self-conscious embarrassment as he regaled his subordinates with a very tiresome secondhand account of her exploits. Having completed his task, he held the horse while Peter handed Susannah up into the vehicle and climbed in after her.

"Although, if Miss is half as handy at driving as she is in the saddle, I shouldn't wonder if you hadn't ought to give her the reins," he added for Peter's benefit.

"An excellent notion," Peter said with a rather forced smile, and offered to surrender the reins to his passenger.

Susannah, much abashed, shook her head vehemently.

"Very well, then, I daresay I shall contrive to keep us out of the ditch." He nodded for the groom to stand back, and soon they were tooling their way down the long drive, leaving Ramsay Hall and its residents behind them.

"I'm sorry," Susannah said, finding her tongue at last. "I should never have pressed you. Only it looked like fun—and indeed it was!—but I never meant for anyone to be hurt."

"Of course you didn't," Peter said soothingly. "As for anyone being hurt, whoever would have guessed that Cousin Jane, of all people, would attempt such a thing?"

"Then you think she fell while sliding down the banister?" demanded Susannah, pleased to know he shared her own theory about Miss Hawthorne's accident.

"I think she must have done, else why would Richard have given you that quelling look, when he feared you were about to say so? And I must say," he added with a kindling eye, "I think it dam—er, dashed unjust of Richard to lay the blame at your door! It's not as if you forced her to do it—nor did you force me, for that matter," he added ruefully.

"No, but if we had not done it first, I doubt if it would have ever occurred to her, for she is such a fine lady. She's everything a baroness should be—and everything I'm not."

"Nonsense!" Peter objected with perhaps more vehemence than veracity.

"It's true, Peter. You know it is!" She heaved a sigh. "I'm never going to fit in here."

"You will—you have only to give yourself time."

She looked up at him doubtfully. "Do you really think so?"

He transferred the reins to one hand so that he might lay the other over hers and give it a reassuring squeeze. "I know so."

She gave him a weak smile. "I'm not sure I believe you, but it's nice of you to say it all the same."

They arrived at the vicarage a short time later, and Peter introduced his American cousin to the vicar, his wife, their three daughters, and a handsome brunette who proved to be their visiting niece. Susannah, whose experience with the clergy was limited to the childless missionary couple who had accompanied her aboard the *Concordia* and the Methodist circuit rider who occasionally enjoyed the hospitality of her father's house as he made his solitary rounds, was charmed by the large and happy Cummings family—a delightful state of affairs that lasted only until Lydia, a bouncing lass of fifteen, giggled behind her hand and inquired archly as to whether an interesting announcement was shortly to be made concerning Susannah and her aristocratic cousin.

"Lydia Cummings!" her mother exclaimed, appalled. "What kind of talk is that?"

"I can't imagine why else Miss Ramsay should have travelled all the way across the ocean," pointed out Lydia in her own defense.

"No, I daresay you can't, for you haven't the least delicacy of mind." Mrs. Cummings informed her roundly, then turned to Susannah with an apologetic smile. "Pray forgive my daughter, Miss Ramsay. My eldest, Amanda, is to go to London in the spring for her come-out, and my silly girls can think of nothing but courtship, and beaux, and marriage."

"Oh, Mama!" protested the eldest Miss Cummings, blushing to the roots of her blonde hair.

"*I* can," put in thirteen-year-old Mary. "If I were going to London, I should much rather see the horses at Astley's Amphitheatre than be courted by a bunch of horrid gentlemen!"

"That's put me in my place," Peter said meekly, although his eyes twinkled.

"Not you, Mr. Ramsay!" Mary insisted, between peals of laughter. "You know I wasn't talking about you!"

"Worse and worse!" cried Peter. "Do you mean to say I'm not horrid, or I'm not a gentleman?"

"You are not horrid at all, and if I had to marry someone, I would rather marry you than anyone else."

"Why, Miss Mary, you unman me!" declared Peter. "Unfortunately, I'm afraid that by the time you come out, your eyes will have been opened, and another will replace me in your esteem."

Mary might have argued the point, had her mother not judged it time to intervene. "If you insist upon putting poor Mr. Ramsay to the blush, Mary, I think it is high time you returned to the schoolroom." Seeing Lydia eyeing her uncertainly, she added, "You may remain, Lydia, if you think you can behave like a lady."

Lydia hastily assured her mother of her ability in this regard and, as the Reverend Mr. Cummings excused himself, citing the need to prepare for his sermon, the party was reduced to Peter and Susannah, Mrs. Cummings, the two elder Cummings girls, and Miss Elizabeth Hunsford, the daughter of Mrs. Cummings's sister. It was this last to whom Peter now addressed himself.

"I understand Miss Cummings is to be brought out by her aunt. Would that be your mother, Miss Hunsford?"

"Yes. Papa and Mama have no acquaintances in London, so they are to bring Cousin Amanda out in exchange for letters of introduction from Aunt

Cummings to all her Society friends."

"You make it sound as if I am bosom-bows with half the aristocracy," protested Mrs. Cummings, laughing. "It is no such thing, but over the years I have kept up correspondence with several ladies who I think will not balk at sending out cards to my sister and her charges."

"And after they meet her," put in Lydia, "Cousin Elizabeth is certain to be asked everywhere, for her dowry is *enormous*!"

Mrs. Cummings frowned. "That's as may be, Lydia, but as to why you should consider it a good thing to be pursued by fortune-hunters—well, I fear your logic quite escapes me."

"Oh, but surely it is better to be pursued by fortune-hunters than not to be pursued by any gentlemen at all!"

"If you think that, it only shows how ill-prepared you are to enter Society," her mother informed her in dampening tones. "I can only hope you will learn wisdom over the next two years, if you think to make your own come-out."

"Yes, for I can assure you it is not pleasant at all to wonder if a gentleman truly likes you, or only hopes to enrich himself by marrying you," Susannah said.

"Very true, Miss Ramsay," Miss Hunsford said,

regarding the American girl with interest. "Am I to understand, then, that you are an heiress yourself?"

"My father left me a large property in Kentucky." Seeing nothing but blank stares on the faces of the three young ladies, she felt compelled to explain. "The American frontier, you know."

"Oh, the wilderness," Miss Hunsford said with what Susannah thought was a rather dismissive nod.

"Have you ever seen a red Indian, Miss Ramsay?" Lydia asked.

"Well, last winter I shot at one who was trying to steal our horses," Susannah confessed. "Still, he was quite far away, so I don't know if he was actually an Indian or merely disguised as one to divert suspicion."

"Did you kill him?" demanded Lydia, wide-eyed.

"No. In fact, I don't think I hit him at all, but the sound of gunfire was sufficient to frighten him off."

Miss Hunsford shuddered. "I should have been quite terrified! It seems to me, Miss Ramsay, that you must be as much a man as you are a woman."

Peter, recalling his American cousin bathing in the lake, could not have agreed with this assessment had Susannah shot a dozen red Indians. Miss Hunsford noticed the thoughtful frown creasing his brow and, reading in it the same disapproval writ large on her Aunt Cummings's countenance, added quickly, "I meant only that you must be the bravest female of my acquaintance, Miss Ramsay. Me, I am so timid I should have to have a man to protect me."

This last was said with a coy glance in Peter's direction, clearly an invitation for him to volunteer his services to Miss Hunsford in this capacity. But since he showed no sign of picking up the verbal glove she had let fall, it was perhaps fortunate that Lydia spoke up, sparing him the necessity.

"It is a good thing you sent Mary back to the schoolroom, Mama, for she would insist upon badgering Miss Ramsay with questions. Depend upon it, Miss Ramsay, you will be her new heroine!"

"I can't imagine why I should be anyone's heroine," Susannah protested. "Miss Hunsford is right, you know; I'm not very ladylike at all, and I always manage to do the wrong thing. If Mary wants a heroine, she should look to Jane—Miss Hawthorne, that is—for she is exactly what a lady ought to be." At her own mention of Jane Hawthorne, Susannah recalled the reason for their visit and turned to Mrs. Cummings. "Oh, I almost forgot! Peter and I are here at her behest, ma'am, for she bade me bring you the receipt you wanted. She would have brought it herself, but she, er, suffered an accident."

"An accident?" Mrs. Cummings echoed in real

alarm. "Why, what happened?"

Susannah fumbled in her reticule for the receipt, and thus avoided Mrs. Cummings's eye. "She, er, fell on the stairs."

"Oh, dear! I trust she is not seriously injured. How did it happen?"

"Er—"

Seeing Susannah floundering for an answer, Peter came to her rescue. "Neither Miss Ramsay nor I were present when it took place, so we cannot say for certain. Thankfully, there appear to be no bones broken, but she must stay off her ankle for a few days."

They left a short time later, amidst emphatic promises from the vicar's wife to call upon the invalid. Although Mrs. Cummings's concern was no doubt real, Susannah found herself hoping that she would make the promised call alone. In all honesty, she could not say she found the vicarage girls agreeable, in spite of their nearness to her own age. She thought Miss Amanda Cummings insipid, and Miss Lydia silly. Even little Miss Mary, who seemed to feel just as she ought on the subject of marriage, was nevertheless brazenly outspoken at an age when, as everyone knew, children were to be seen and not heard; Susannah only hoped that by the time that damsel made her own come-out four or five years hence, Peter would be married or otherwise safely removed from her grasp. As for the vicar's niece, Miss Hunsford, she was the worst of all— a simpering ninny who apparently thought her dowry would have every man in London falling at her feet. That it was in fact Miss Lydia and not Miss Hunsford who had voiced such a prediction in no way altered Susannah's opinion of the heiress.

13

A vain man may become proud
and imagine himself pleasing to all
when he is in reality a universal nuisance.
BENEDICT [BARUCH] SPINOZA, *Ethics*

O ver the next several days, the residents of
Ramsay Hall struggled to find a new
equilibrium. The groom fashioned a crutch for
Jane, and by leaning her weight upon it, she was able to
hobble from room to room. Climbing the stairs was
quite another matter, so one of the salons on the ground
floor had been fitted out as a temporary bedchamber.
Susannah assumed charge of the staff, at first merely
relaying Jane's orders, but later, as her confidence
grew, venturing to issue instructions of her own. With
the running of the household in her American cousin's
increasingly capable hands, Jane spent most of her time
in the drawing room, either resting on the sofa with her
ankle elevated or sitting at the small rosewood desk

writing out cards of invitation to the ball which would be held in two weeks' time. In spite of the myriad tasks to be completed before this event, Jane was determined to follow the physician's instructions to the letter so that she might be back on her feet in time for the ball— not that she had any expectation of enjoying this celebration of the death of her hopes; in fact, she was quite determined that her interesting (and inexplicable) injury should not usurp the attention that rightfully belonged to Susannah.

Indeed, she was already getting far more attention than she wished. The Aunts walked up from the Dower House every morning, usually bearing a black bottle of some noxious potion from Aunt Charlotte's stillroom which, they assured her, would have her back on her feet before the cat could lick her ear. Jane accepted these medicaments with expressions of gratitude, then tipped them into a potted plant as soon as the Aunts' backs were turned. (The fact that one of these plants died within forty-eight hours after receiving such a treatment was a source of much hilarity amongst the residents of Ramsay Hall.)

Jane only wished she could deal in so cavalier a manner with Sir Matthew Pitney. Alas, once word of her indisposition reached Pitney Grange, Jane's ardent suitor had lost no time in paying his respects, bearing with him an armload of flowers which, she thought, must have utterly denuded his gardens. In this supposition she proved to be mistaken, for he appeared in the drawing room every day with a similar offering, expressing his fervent wishes for her good health, and his conviction that such an accident never would have occurred had she been safely housed beneath his own roof.

"Of that, Sir Matthew, I am certain," she murmured, determinedly avoiding the gaze of Richard, who glowered at his neighbor from a wingchair on the opposite side of Jane's sofa.

Sir Matthew, surprised and gratified by her unexpected agreement, might have pressed his suit in spite of Lord Ramsay's rather daunting presence, had the butler not appeared at that moment to announce a bevy of new callers.

"Mrs. Cummings, Miss Cummings, Miss Lydia Cummings, and Miss Hunsford," Wilson proclaimed, then stepped back to allow the vicar's wife and her charges to enter.

"How kind of you to call," Jane began, struggling to sit upright and thus make room for at least two of the newcomers at the other end of the sofa.

"No, Jane, stay where you are." Richard rose and offered his chair to Mrs. Cummings, and Sir Matthew was quick to follow his example. "Wilson, bring chairs from the dining room—and the tea tray, if you please."

Any hopes Jane might have entertained that Sir Matthew would take his leave with the influx of new callers died when the additional chairs were brought and he planted himself in the one nearest her head.

"Your cousin Miss Ramsay told me you had fallen on the stairs," Mrs. Cummings said, accepting Jane's invitation to pour out the tea. "I was never more shocked!"

"Where is Miss Ramsay, anyway?" piped up Lydia, taking a cup of tea from her mother's hand and bearing it precariously across the room to Sir Matthew.

"She and Mr. Ramsay have gone out riding," Jane said. "He had to see to the thatching of one of the cottages, and has taken her along to introduce her to some of the tenants. I daresay they will return shortly."

The vicar's wife nodded in approval. "A capable young man, and a very pretty-behaved one, too."

"Most of the time," Richard muttered under his breath.

The young man in question looked into the drawing room a short time later accompanied by Susannah, the latter looking charmingly windblown in a stylish riding habit of bottle green velvet which had been delivered by his lordship's tailor only that morning, said tailor having been paid a premium to complete this order ahead of several other projects.

"I beg your pardon, Cousin Jane," Peter said, drawing up short at the sight of no fewer than three young ladies giggling up at him. "I didn't know you were entertaining callers. If you will excuse me, ladies, Sir Matthew, I will change out of my riding clothes. Cousin Susannah, you had best do the same."

He took a step backward, but was forestalled by a chorus of female protests. "Pray don't go on our account, Mr. Ramsay," objected Miss Cummings, speaking for the group. "Surely you need not stand upon ceremony with such old friends as we are."

"I daresay I can claim a longstanding friendship with you and your sisters, Miss Cummings, but I have only just met your cousin," Peter pointed out. "I should hate to prejudice Miss Hunsford against me by sitting down in all my dirt."

"And how are we to further our acquaintance, Mr. Ramsay, if you insist upon spending all your time changing clothes?" Miss Hunsford asked, smiling coyly up at him in a way that, to one pair of eyes at least, somehow appeared both demure and predatory at the same time.

For Susannah was experiencing a most unwelcome epiphany. That unlikeliest of possibilities, that an unattached heiress should appear in rural Hampshire, had apparently come to pass—and the heiress in question appeared to take more than a passing interest in Peter's *beaux yeux*. Since Miss Hunsford would not be travelling to London until the spring, he would have plenty of time to fix his interest with her before the more comfortably circumstanced gentlemen of the *ton* would give him any competition. It seemed to Susannah that he might be able to achieve his dream of becoming master of Fairacres after all. Surely anyone who claimed friendship with Peter must be happy for him; why, then, did she suddenly feel like scratching the heiress's eyes out?

She shook off the question for which she could find no satisfactory answer, and focused her attention on the conversation just in time to hear Mrs. Cummings address Jane.

"I'm sure this forced inactivity must be difficult for you, Miss Hawthorne," the vicar's wife was saying. "You are not the sort to be content with idleness."

"No, indeed I am not! Fortunately, Miss Ramsay has been invaluable as far as the daily running of the household is concerned, so I need have no concerns on that head." She glanced at the little pile of vellum cards on the writing desk. "But I have not been idle, for there is to be a ball in two weeks' time to introduce Miss

Ramsay to the neighborhood gentry, and I have been making out the invitations. You may expect to receive one within the next few days; do say you and Mr. Cummings will accept, and bring Miss Cummings and Miss Hunsford."

Mrs. Cummings glanced uncertainly at her elder daughter and niece. "Certainly we would love to attend. I don't doubt it will do the girls a great deal of good to break in their dancing slippers, so to speak, at a country ball before they are presented in London next spring. I only hope their lack of experience in such matters will not make you regret extending your kind invitation."

"Not at all," Jane assured her. "In fact, Miss Ramsay shares their dilemma, so I have conceived the notion of having a small party one afternoon next week to allow the young people to practice their dancing before the event. I had hoped to make up one of the set myself, but since Dr. Calloway forbids it, I wonder if you would allow Miss Lydia to take my place. It is not like a formal ball," she added quickly, anticipating the objections inherent in issuing such an invitation to a young lady not yet out in Society, "and I should not press you to allow it if you cannot like the idea. But it would, as you say, allow Miss Lydia to gain a little experience in such situations before she makes her own come-out in a few years, and, well, I should be very much obliged to you."

"Oh, do say I may, Mama!" begged Lydia, bouncing up and down on her chair in excitement.

"Hush, child, and be still, lest you demonstrate to Miss Hawthorne just how unprepared you are to make such appearances." Having reduced her middle daughter to anguished silence, she turned back to Jane. "I cannot agree to such a thing without discussing it first with my husband. Still, he is usually guided by me in matters concerning the girls, and I suppose I can have no objection, since your injury will leave you one female short of a set otherwise."

Lydia collapsed against the back of her chair, heaving a sigh of patent relief. Sir Matthew, seeing this, chuckled.

"I hope I am to be invited to this party as well, Miss Hawthorne. If not, I shall be quite as devastated as Miss Lydia, should our good vicar deny her such a treat."

"Why, you are welcome to come, Sir Matthew, if that is what you wish," Jane said, surprised and not at all pleased. "But it is to be little more than a school-room party, you know. I fear you will be shockingly bored."

"I am sure no man could be bored in the midst of so much feminine beauty," declared Sir Matthew to the room at large, then bent an avuncular smile upon Lydia. "Although I'm sure I must seem quite ancient to Miss Lydia here, I hope she will honour me with a dance."

Lydia giggled at the novelty of being solicited for a dance just as if she were a grown up lady, but (it must be noted) made no attempt to deny the charge even as she agreed to Sir Matthew's request.

The matter of the dancing party being settled, Peter and Susannah excused themselves to their respective rooms to change clothes and the vicarage party soon took their leave, punctuated by urgings by Mrs. Cummings that Miss Hawthorne was to send to the vicarage should she find herself in need of anything its inhabitants could provide. The door had hardly closed behind them when Richard rose from his chair.

"I hope you will not think me shockingly rude, Sir Matthew," he began, although a more astute listener than Sir Matthew might have been aware that nothing in Lord Ramsay's voice or bearing indicated great concern on his part, "but it is obvious all this enter-taining has exhausted Miss Hawthorne. I think we must bid you good day now."

"What? Oh, yes, of course. I should not like to think of poor Miss Hawthorne suffering on my account. I shall take my leave at once, and hope to find you in better spirits tomorrow."

"Thank you, Sir Matthew," Jane said, offering her hand.

He bowed himself from the room with disjointed apologies for disturbing Miss Hawthorne's peace and promises to call again upon the morrow, if he had not utterly worn out his welcome that afternoon.

"Impossible," Richard told Jane once they were alone. "His welcome was worn out years ago."

She smiled at this assertion, but made no attempt to dispute it. "Poor Sir Matthew! I could almost feel sorry for him, being dismissed so summarily. So I am 'exhausted' by the simple act of taking tea with fewer than half a dozen neighbors? I hope I am not so frail a creature!"

"Perhaps not, but you cannot tell me you are not tired, for I have only to look at your eyes to know better," he said with mock severity.

"And now you are telling me I look hag-ridden!" Jane chided him. "It is no such thing, but I confess I did not sleep well last night. The sofa is comfortable enough, but it cannot take the place of my own bed."

"In that case, you shall lie on your own bed."

He took her hands and pulled her to her feet. Recognizing that it would be pointless to argue, she positioned the crutch under her arm.

"You realize, of course, that by the time I make it

all the way up the stairs with my crutch, it will be time to come down again."

"*Damn* your crutch."

He pulled it from beneath her arm and tossed it to the floor, then swept her up in his arms.

"Ah, there you are, Wilson," he said, seeing the butler standing in the hall goggling at them. "I am taking Miss Hawthorne up to her room to rest. Pray have her woman attend her there."

"Er, yes, my lord," said Wilson, and promptly made himself scarce.

"Richard!" Jane protested, half laughing as he started up the stairs. "Put me down at once!"

"I will put you down on your own bed, and not one moment before. Now, stop struggling before I lose my balance and fall, and then we will *both* be laid up lame—and *that*, I fear, would be rather difficult to explain to the neighbors."

"Yes, Richard," she said meekly, and allowed herself the luxury of resting her head on his shoulder.

It was rather ironic, she thought, that he could be so attuned to her physical condition as to be able to look into her eyes and know she was tired, and yet be wholly oblivious to the state of her heart. And a very good thing, too, she reminded herself sternly, or it would have been most uncomfortable for both of them, being obliged as they were to live beneath the same roof. Still, she wished he might be less considerate, less concerned for her comfort. For with every such demonstration, it only grew harder to face the prospect of giving him up.

14

Yes, I'm in love, I feel it now
And Caelia has undone me;
And yet I swear I can't tell how
The pleasing plague stole on me.
WILLIAM WHITEHEAD, *The Je ne sçay quoi song*

*T*he day of the dancing-party dawned cloudy with a promise of rain in the air, but within the walls of Ramsay Hall, spirits were high in spite of the gloomy weather. Susannah had progressed in her lessons to the point where, instead of viewing the exercise with dread, she actually looked forward to the opportunity to put her newly acquired skills to the test. Peter expressed his intention of catching up on his work before the guests arrived, and so spent the morning shut up in his office, but the yoke of his labours was apparently light, for snatches of cheerful whistling could sometimes be heard issuing from this chamber. Richard, for his part, determined not only to send his carriage for the Aunts lest they be caught in the rain while making the trek from the Dower House on foot, but to go himself and offer the elderly ladies his escort. Jane, while still not up to dancing, was now able to walk short distances without the aid of her crutch, and could even mount the stairs by leaning heavily on the same banister that had once proved her undoing. All in all, she thought there was much to be said for a small, informal party. She suspected the mood would be quite different on the night of the formal betrothal ball a se'ennight hence; she knew her own sentiments on that occasion would be far from cheerful.

These suspicions were further bolstered by the appearance of Susannah in the music room. Of course, ballroom attire would be highly inappropriate for an impromptu party of this sort, but the girl was disturbingly appealing nonetheless in one of her new morning gowns, this one of green sprigged muslin that emphasized her trim, rounded figure and brought out the coppery highlights in her hair. Peter, rigged out in a double-breasted blue tailcoat that would not have shamed Old Bond Street, bowed deeply before her.

"I hope you will do me the honour of standing up with me for the waltz, Miss Ramsay," he said.

"The honour will be all mine, sir," she said, sinking into an exaggerated curtsy.

"Trying to steal a march on me, are you, Peter?"

Both young people turned toward the door and beheld Lord Ramsay, resplendent in a mulberry tailcoat of Bath superfine, framed in the aperture.

"As if I could, Richard!" Peter retorted, grinning. "Have you brought the Aunts, then? Aunt Charlotte, Aunt Amelia, how very fine you look! You put us all to shame."

"How gallant of you to say so, Peter!" exclaimed Aunt Amelia, blushing like a schoolgirl.

Aunt Charlotte, whose mind was of more practical a bent, merely shook her head. "If you think that, Peter, it only confirms what I had suspected: the lighting in this room is insufficient for a morning function, for it will not have full sun until the afternoon."

"In that case, we shall have the candles lit," promised Richard, and rang for a servant.

The answer to this summons came, however, not from the footman, but from Wilson, who paused in the doorway with Sir Matthew at his heels. "Sir Matthew Pitney," he announced.

Sir Matthew made his bows, then charted a direct course for the place where Jane sat against the wall on a striped satin sofa. "My dear Miss Hawthorne, I hope I find you sufficiently improved to perform the waltz with me."

"Alas, no, Sir Matthew. That is, I am improving,

and can now walk a little without using a crutch, but I fear dancing is still beyond me. I am being very careful to follow Dr. Calloway's instructions, in the hopes that I might be able to dance at our ball. I trust you received the invitation I sent?"

"I did indeed, and I share your hope that you will be able to dance by that time." He leaned nearer and lowered his voice to a conspiratorial whisper. "In anticipation of that happy outcome, may I request that you honour me with the first waltz? I confess, I am deeply resentful of the accident that robbed me of the opportunity to hold you in my arms."

Jane, recalling that in the aftermath of that accident she had been held far more literally in the arms of another, blushed crimson. "You must not speak so, Sir Matthew. As for my granting you the first waltz, I should hate to make such a promise and then be unable to keep it. If I were to agree to such a request, and then be obliged to sit against the wall—"

"In such a case, I should consider it a pleasure to sit with you," promised her swain. "But I see that I have said too much, although your charming blushes encourage me to hope."

"Really, Sir Matthew, I don't—"

Jane's protests were interrupted by the arrival of the vicarage party, and although Aunt Charlotte might scowl her disapproval at the boisterousness of the giddy trio of girls who entered the drawing room in Mrs. Cummings's wake, Jane would willingly have fallen on their necks in gratitude.

"I fear you have a great deal to answer for, Miss Hawthorne," chided the vicar's wife with a twinkle in her eye. "This morning at breakfast, I made the observation that it looked like rain and wondered aloud whether this party would be better postponed. I have never heard such a display of filial disobedience in all my life! Anyone listening would have supposed I had threatened to confine the girls to their rooms with only bread and water."

"I am very glad you brought the girls in spite of your misgivings, for I am persuaded there is no need for concern," Jane told her, rising gingerly from the sofa to greet them. "My gardener says the rain will not arrive until later tonight, and he is right about these things more often than not."

"No, no, Miss Hawthorne, you need not get up," objected Mrs. Cummings. "As to the weather, I daresay your gardener is quite correct. It has often been my observation that those who work closely with God's creation seem to have an unusual instinct for such matters."

"And if inclement weather should indeed threaten,

I shall send you all home in my carriage," promised Richard.

"I hope you will permit Mr. Ramsay to accompany us," Miss Hunsford put in, smiling coyly at Peter. "I am quite terrified of thunder and lightning, you know, and there is something so comforting about a man's presence."

"Am I to understand then, Miss Hunsford, that you consider my cousin more suited to fill this rôle than I am?" inquired Richard with a twinkle in his eye.

"Oh, my!" exclaimed the heiress, all aflutter. "I meant no such thing, my lord. I only thought, well, a baron must have a hundred things to do more important than escorting a carriage full of females home through a thunderstorm."

Richard nodded in understanding. "Whereas Mr. Ramsay has nothing more than the administration of a large estate to occupy his attention."

"Just so!" agreed Miss Hunsford brightly, oblivious to irony.

"You hear that, Peter? In case of inclement weather, I shall depend on you."

Peter nodded. "I shall almost hope for rain, then, so that I might have some way of filling the empty hours."

"And now I think you are roasting me, Mr. Ramsay," Miss Hunsford chided him playfully, rapping him on the arm with her folded fan.

"Indeed I am, Miss Hunsford," he confessed. "I trust you will forgive me."

"Only if you will stand up with me at Miss Ramsay's ball next week."

"Elizabeth!" cried Mrs. Cummings, scandalized. "I don't know how things are done in the West Indies, but here it is for a gentleman to ask a lady to dance, not the other way 'round. If you don't wish to give all the gentlemen a disgust of you, you would do well to remember it."

"Oh dear!" Miss Hunsford turned large brown eyes on Peter. "Is it true, Mr. Ramsay?"

"In general, yes," he confessed apologetically. "But I cannot regret your ignorance, if it means I am to have the honour of leading you onto the floor."

The vicar's wife gave a nod of approval. "Very prettily said, Mr. Ramsay. But I fear, Elizabeth, that you may not find London gentlemen so understanding."

Thankfully for Miss Hunsford, she was spared a scold by the return of the butler, this time to announce the arrival of young Mr. Charles Langley, scion of a local landowner, who was down from Oxford on holiday, and who would make up the fourth and final gentleman of the set.

"Good morning, Mr. Langley," Jane said, extending her hand to him. "I am so glad you could join us."

"Not at all," the young man demurred, flushing. "What I mean is, do me good to get in a bit of practice before jogging up to London for a bit of Town-bronze, what?"

"Very true," Jane agreed, smiling. "You will find the young ladies of the party in very similar circumstances, so I hope you can all help one another. Aunt Amelia, we are all assembled now, so if you will take your place at the pianoforte, we will begin."

The party paired off, with Richard leading Susannah into the set. Peter offered his arm to Miss Hunsford (who looked to Susannah's eyes like the cat that ate the canary), while Sir Matthew reluctantly left Jane's side to bow before Miss Cummings, leaving Miss Lydia and Mr. Langley to make up the fourth couple in the set.

Aunt Charlotte, for her part, seated herself next to Jane on the sofa, from which vantage point she might observe the dancers and offer criticism or, less often, praise.

"Mr. Langley, if you will stay with the beat, perhaps Miss Lydia will not feel the need to drag you about the floor," she barked at the vicar's younger daughter and her partner. "Susannah, do try to relax.

His lordship will not bite you. Peter, Miss Hunsford, you make a very handsome couple, I must say."

This observation could hardly be said to have helped Susannah relax. Instead, she tried to rise up on tiptoe in order to watch Peter and his partner over the shoulder of her betrothed, while at the same time not losing the beat of the music.

"What is the matter, Susannah?" asked Richard, frowning at these not entirely successful maneuvers.

"Nothing, only the—the sun is in my eyes."

Richard's own eyes widened a little at this assertion since, as Aunt Charlotte had noted, the morning sun had not yet penetrated the morning room windows.

After what seemed to Susannah an interminably long time, Aunt Amelia pounded out the final chords. The four couples separated, and all the dancers bowed or curtsied to their partners, then dispersed and began to re-form for the next set.

"If you will do me the honour, Miss Ramsay?"

Susannah was vaguely disappointed to see Mr. Langley bowing deeply before her. "Thank you, sir," she said, summoning up a smile as she answered his bow with a curtsy.

She soon discovered why Miss Lydia Cummings had felt the need to drag her partner about the floor. Mr.

Langley performed the steps apparently at random, the only evidence that he kept any sort of count at all discernable in the fact that he marked the first beat of every measure by treading squarely upon her toe. If the previous dance had been distressing for reasons she could not quite define, this one was quite literally painful. Susannah could not quite stifle her sigh of relief when it finally came to an end. She was wondering if she might plead fatigue and sit the next one out when Peter approached and took her arm.

"Do say you will rescue me from Miss Hunsford, Cousin Susannah," he urged in hushed tones. "She has been dropping the most flagrant hints for the waltz, and I dare not rebuff her without appearing shockingly rude."

"Oh, is the next dance to be a waltz, then?" Susannah remembered her disappointment at not being allowed to waltz with Peter during her lessons, but now that the opportunity had presented itself to her, she felt awkward and ill at ease. Still, if the only alternative was to sit beside Jane and Aunt Charlotte and watch as he attempted to fend off the predatory heiress . . . She gave a decisive nod, the pain in her toes forgotten. "Very well, Peter."

"I stand forever in your debt," Peter said gratefully, and took her in the hold she had practiced so often with

Richard.

Her breath caught in her throat. It had never felt like this with Richard. Her betrothed was quite tall, and when he had held her thus, his close proximity had afforded her nothing more than an excellent view of his cravat. Peter, however, was rather shorter, and she had only to lift her chin slightly to look straight into his dark eyes. Furthermore, she could feel the heat emanating from his body, and the awareness made her face grow warm. She lowered her gaze under the guise of minding her steps.

"I should think you would want to encourage Miss Hunsford," she observed somewhat breathlessly under the cover of the music. "Her dowry would allow you to purchase Fairacres."

Peter addressed himself to the top of her downcast head. "I don't think I could bring myself to marry a lady only for her dowry, even for Fairacres. Nor, for that matter, do I think she has the slightest interest in marriage to me. Depend upon it, I am nothing more than a convenient target upon which to practice her charms prior to her brilliant London debut."

"In that case, I wish she would focus her attention on Richard," she grumbled.

"Perhaps she assumes, like you, that my rather precarious position in Society renders me uniquely susceptible to the charms of well-dowered young ladies," he suggested.

"I'm sure I never said—"

"Or," he continued, "perhaps she has taken Miss Lydia's hints to heart, and deduced, quite rightly, that Richard belongs to you."

"To *me*?" echoed Susannah.

"It is you to whom he is promised to marry," Peter pointed out reasonably. "If you are concerned about his breaking faith with you, I can assure you that you need not be. Miss Hunsford is surely aware of this, and has therefore set her sights on my humble self. I suppose I must be flattered that she found me preferable to Sir Matthew or Mr. Langley."

Susannah made no reply to this sally, but glanced over his shoulder at the subject of their conversation. Miss Hunsford was now partnered with Lord Ramsay, and as Susannah watched her twirling about the room in the arms of her own betrothed, the heiress looked up and laughed at something he had said. It was very strange, really. From the moment Lord Ramsay's letter had reached her in Kentucky, she had indulged in glorious dreams of arriving in England to discover that the man she had accepted sight unseen was in fact the embodiment of her every romantic fantasy. And sure enough, after that first unfortunate meeting, Richard had proven to be just the sort of man with whom any young lady might fall deeply in love.

What she had not expected, what she could never have anticipated, was that she would fall deeply in love with his steward instead.

15

Even such a man, so faint, so spiritless,
So dull, so dead in look, so woe-begone,
Drew Priam's curtain in the dead of night,
And would have told him half his Troy was burned.
WILLIAM SHAKESPEARE, *King Henry the Fourth*

*I*t was a pleasantly weary Ramsay family that assembled around the dinner table that evening. Conversation was lively, for the morning's dancing-party must be discussed in detail, with Susannah congratulated on all sides for her performance, and Peter roasted roundly for being the object of Miss Hunsford's amorous interest. From the dancing-party to the approaching ball required only a step, but here, it must be noted, the discussion lost much of its liveliness. Susannah lapsed into un-characteristic silence, while Jane appeared pale and tense, Peter grew thoughtful, and Richard, at the head of the table, voiced his opinions with tight-lipped stoicism. When a flash of lightning briefly illuminated the room, followed by the rumble of thunder, the younger members of the party seized with gratitude upon the opportunity to turn the subject.

"It appears you will need to send the Aunts home in your carriage after all, Richard," Peter observed.

"It does, indeed," he concurred.

"Oh, would you, Richard dear?" pleaded Aunt Amelia. "I hate to ask you to send your coachman out in this weather, to say nothing of your poor horses, but I cannot like the thought of walking back to the Dower House."

Aunt Charlotte glanced toward the window, which rattled with the force of the raindrops against the glass. "I have always been of the opinion that a little rain never hurt anyone, but I can't say I would care to walk home in this storm, either," she remarked.

"There is no question of your doing so," insisted Richard. "Of course, there is a third alternative. You are free to stay here until the storm subsides, if you wish."

"I should not like to put you to any trouble," objected Aunt Amelia without much conviction.

"It is no trouble at all," Jane put in. "If you should care to spend the night and return to the Dower House in the morning, the rose saloon can be prepared for you in a trice."

"Well—" dithered Aunt Amelia, glancing

uncertainly at the window, "if you are quite sure—"

Before she could finish the thought, the door to the dining room burst open. All eyes turned to see Wilson, clearly labouring under some strong emotion, framed therein.

"Begging your pardon, my lord—ladies—" he began disjointedly. "It's the physician. He says—"

The physician, it seemed, was perfectly capable of speaking for himself. Mr. Calloway brushed past the butler and addressed Richard. "It was a lightning strike, my lord. I was just passing by on my way home from a call when I saw it. Send every able-bodied man you can spare to fight the fire, for it would be disastrous if the flames were to reach the Home Wood."

Richard was on his feet in an instant. "Yes, but *what* was struck by lightning? Talk sense, man!"

"Fairacres," Mr. Calloway said. "The old manor house is ablaze."

Susannah looked at Peter, and found him sitting as if turned to stone. "Peter?" she called softly.

"We'll be there at once," Richard promised. "See to it, will you, Peter? Doctor, I would be obliged to you if you could hold yourself in readiness to treat anyone who might be injured in fighting the fire."

"Of course, my lord, but if you've no objection, I should like to ride to the vicarage first, and have Mr.

Cummings organize a second party of men."

Richard nodded. "Yes, an excellent notion."

Susannah jerked to her feet like a puppet on a string. "You will need us to have hot water and bandages ready, won't you, Doctor? And Cousin Jane, we had best make sure there is refreshment for the firefighters—coffee, perhaps, and sandwiches. They may have a long night ahead of them."

Everyone at the table stared speechlessly at their American relation's cool assumption of authority— everyone except Peter, who managed a strained smile. "Thank you," he murmured.

"Cousin Susannah is quite right," Jane pronounced, finding her tongue at last. "Richard, Peter, you must lose no time. If you cannot save Fairacres, at least you can ensure that the fire does not spread. We ladies will be in the kitchen, if you should have need of us. Come along, Aunt Charlotte, Aunt Amelia."

Jane shepherded the Aunts from the dining room in the wake of Susannah, who had already disappeared through the door and was no doubt halfway to the kitchen.

"Thank you, Jane. Wilson," his lordship addressed the butler, "go below stairs and collect every man-servant who can be spared. Peter, run to the stables and have the groom hitch up two wagons—one to convey the pump to the river, the other to carry the men. While you are there, saddle Diablo for me and Sheba for yourself. I shall join you there directly."

"Of course." Peter cast his napkin aside and rose from the table, pausing only long enough to take one last quick gulp of wine from his glass before setting out for the stables.

He soon discovered that the news had preceded him, for the stables were in an uproar; he realized belatedly that the stable hand who had taken charge of the physician's horse had lost no time in spreading the word.

"Mr. Ramsay, sir, is it true what Jem says about Fairacres?" the groom asked urgently.

"Yes, it's quite true," Peter said. "Even if we can't save the house, we must prevent the flames from reaching the Home Wood. We need a wagon to convey the pump down to the river, and another to carry the men who will soon be—ah, here they come now."

Sure enough, a cacophony of male voices penetrated the stable walls, and a moment later more than a dozen men entered the building, a cross-section of the domestic hierarchy that represented all ranks from the butler down to the youngest pot boy. Peter summoned three of the stoutest footmen to assist him, and the four of them lifted the cumbersome pump and its hoses onto the back of the wagon while the groom hitched the huge draft horses to the traces. Once this task was completed and the wagon sent on its way, Peter ordered the remaining men into the second wagon, which soon departed the stable in the wake of the first.

"Good man!" pronounced Richard a short time later, entering the stable to find his horse saddled and waiting. His voice echoed strangely in the stable, which was empty of all but Peter.

"I sent the others ahead," Peter said, noting that his cousin had taken a moment to change into more serviceable garments. In his own eagerness to save Fairacres, he had set out in his evening clothes, which would probably be ruined long before morning. Still, if only the house might be saved, he would count their loss a price well paid. He turned back to Sheba and gave a last tug to the girth of the saddle. "We should be able to overtake them easily enough."

"Then let us do so."

The two men swung themselves into the saddle and set out at a canter—as fast as they dared over open country in the dark, lest an unseen rabbit hole bring them to grief before they ever reached the blaze.

They saw the smoke rising above the treetops long before the house itself was visible, a billowing black cloud eerily tinged with orange. Peter's breath caught in his throat as they cleared the wood and emerged onto the meadow where he and Susannah had ridden only a couple of weeks earlier. The picturesque manor house was hardly recognizable, replaced instead by a scene straight from the pits of hell. Flames shot forty feet into the air, casting into silhouette the figures of the men who had dismounted from the wagon so that they looked like demons dancing about a bonfire. Richard flung himself from the saddle and tied his terrified mount at a safe distance, looping the reins loosely in case their efforts at containing the blaze should fail and the horse should have to be removed quickly. His actions jolted Peter out of his horrified trance, and he quickly followed his cousin's example, looping Sheba's reins about a low-hanging tree limb as he murmured calming words—although whether these were intended to comfort his horse or himself, he could not have said.

Once on the scene, Richard lost no time in taking charge, shouting to make himself heard over the roar and crackle of the conflagration as he oversaw the unloading of the pump. Peter, not content to operate in a purely advisory capacity, grabbed one end of the hose and dragged it down to the river's edge, wading out knee-deep in order to plunge the mouth of the hose well below the surface. If the water was cold, he didn't notice; he was thankful to have some occupation. For surely anything was better than standing about staring helplessly at the inferno that represented the death of all his worldly ambition.

* * *

For the Ramsay ladies, the night was less active, if no less stressful. Upon reaching the kitchen ahead of her cousin and aunts (no difficult task, as two were elderly and the third dependent upon a crutch to aid her in descending the stairs), Susannah snatched a coarse linen apron from a hook on the wall and tied it on over her gown. She spied the two fragrant loaves of bread intended to feed the family the following day and set upon them with a knife, slicing them up and making sandwiches from whatever cold meats and cheeses she could find—an act of vandalism which would surely have enraged Antoine, had he been present to witness it. But, perhaps thankfully, Antoine had been pressed into service as a firefighter—a waste of his talents to which he might have objected strenuously, had he not deemed the prospect of being left out of the excitement a fate far worse.

Alas, having completed this task and overseen the brewing of coffee and the heating of water for any medical needs that might arise, there was very little for Susannah to do but wait and wonder, and recall with vivid clarity the expression on Peter's face when he'd first learned that Fairacres was ablaze.

"You've worked so hard, Susannah," Jane observed, jerked from her own reverie by the sound of the kitchen clock tinnily chiming two. "Perhaps you should lie down. We will wake you when the men return," she added quickly, anticipating the girl's objection, even if she could not fully comprehend its reasons.

Susannah shook her head emphatically. "No, I couldn't. Please don't ask me!"

Jane did not press her, and the ladies lapsed once more into silence.

The sky was just beginning to lighten in the east when the sounds of masculine voices outside, followed by the stamp of footsteps on the stoop, signalled the return of the firefighting brigade. A moment later the door burst open and the kitchen was invaded by men: dirty, sweaty, exhausted men who reeked of smoke.

"Richard!" exclaimed Jane, and it said much for her own emotional state that she forgot to address him by his title in front of the servants. "Is everything all right?"

"Where is Peter?" Susannah asked, searching for his familiar face in the mêlée.

"That depends upon your definition of 'all right.'

Thank you, Aunt Charlotte," Richard said, accepting a steaming cup of coffee from his elderly relation. "The manor house at Fairacres is gone, but we were able to prevent the fire from spreading. The vicar and his party arrived with a second pump, so we used it to saturate the trees bordering the property, containing the blaze until it burned itself out."

"Here, Richard dear, have a sandwich," urged Aunt Amelia, pressing one into his hand.

"Where is Peter?" Susannah asked again.

"Miss Hawthorne," the physician addressed Jane, "I am sorry to report that young George Hastings suffered minor burns on his hands. If you are not worn off your feet already, I wonder if you might assist me in cleaning and treating the wounds."

"Yes, of course," Jane said at once, recognizing the name of Ramsay Hall's second footman. "Bring him here to the table, where the light is better."

There followed a series of difficult maneuvers intended to transfer the suffering footman through the crowded kitchen to the heavy deal table usually reserved for Antoine's use.

"*Where is Peter?*" demanded Susannah, determined not to be ignored any longer.

"Peter?" Richard scanned the teeming kitchen from his superior height. "I don't see him. He was with us when we reached the house; I daresay he must have stopped to clean the mud from his shoes. No doubt he will be along presently."

Susannah did not wait to hear more. She snatched one of the cups of coffee Aunt Charlotte was dispensing, pushed her way through the crowd of men to the door, and opened it. Just as she had expected, Peter sat on the stoop, leaning forward with his elbows resting on his knees and his shoulders slumped in a posture indicative of deepest despair.

"Peter?" she addressed him softly. "I—I've brought you some coffee."

He turned to look up at her, and the sight of him was enough to break her heart. His damp, dark hair was plastered to his scalp, his face was black with soot, and the elegant evening clothes he'd worn at dinner were soaking wet and caked with mud. But all this paled beside the utter hopelessness in his eyes.

"I hope you like it black," she said apologetically, indicating the coffee cup in her hands. "I didn't know what to put in it."

He managed to summon up a bleak smile for her. "Black will do very well. Thank you."

She handed the cup down to him, then gathered her apron-covered skirts and seated herself on the stoop beside him. "I'm sorry about Fairacres, Peter. I know how much it meant to you."

"Oh well," he said with a sigh, "it's unlikely I would have been able to buy it in any case. At least I may now rebuff Miss Hunsford's advances with a clear conscience," he added in a woefully unsuccessful attempt at humour.

"Or you might marry her and buy another property, one that has not lain fallow for decades." Even as she said the words, she hated the thought of Peter caught in the heiress's toils. Still, she would gladly shove Miss Hunsford into his arms herself, if that would erase the misery from his eyes.

He shook his head impatiently. "But that was much of its appeal, don't you see? Anyone could administer Cousin Richard's holdings, vast as they are, because they have been well managed for generations. One has only to continue what others before him have begun. But to take a neglected property, to bring it back to life through one's own efforts—*that* is what I dreamed of doing with Fairacres."

"In fact, you had thought to awaken the Sleeping Beauty with a kiss," she said, falling back upon the fairytale theme they had explored on their earlier visit to Fairacres.

She had the satisfaction of seeing his expression lightened by the faintest hint of a smile. "I suppose you might put it in such fanciful terms—although the analogy breaks down when one considers that to have won the fair 'lady,' I must needs have made a loveless marriage with another, far more literal lady."

"You will find another such property—perhaps one attached to a lady you might bring yourself to love. You have a gift, you know, for seeing what others do not. You see beauty and usefulness where others see nothing but barrenness and neglect." She looked down and fingered the coarse linen of her apron. "You see a lady where others see only wild hair, unfashionable clothes, and peculiar manners."

"That, at least, requires no special gift," he assured her. "I see nothing that has not been there all along, waiting to be discovered."

Her trembling hands pleated the folds of linen covering her lap. "Like—like the Sleeping Beauty, awaiting her prince's kiss?" Her breath came quick and shallow, as if she had run all the way from Fairacres.

"Just so. Susannah—"

She looked up at him, and their eyes met and held. He put his arm around her waist, and then slowly, ever so slowly, leaned toward her until his lips touched hers. She gave a little sigh of surrender, and her warm breath against his mouth emboldened him to tighten his arm about her and kiss her in earnest. He was afterwards to wonder where it might have ended, had a sudden noise from the kitchen not recalled him to his senses.

He jerked upright, releasing his hold on her as if scalded by her touch. "Forgive me—I should not have—" He clambered to his feet and looked down at her with something akin to horror. "I beg your pardon," he said, and disappeared into the kitchen as if the Furies were at his heels.

"Oh, but I wanted you to," she whispered to the empty spot on the stoop where he'd been sitting. "I think I've wanted you to ever since I saw you standing on the dock at Portsmouth."

16

O, Susannah! O, don't you cry for me.
STEPHEN COLLINS FOSTER, *O, Susannah!*

*G*iven the lateness of the hour at which they had finally sought their respective beds, it was hardly surprising that the family did not assemble in the breakfast room until fully noon. Susannah entered the room to find Richard and Jane already there, and after a murmured "good morning," she served herself from the chafing dishes on the sideboard and took a place at the table opposite Jane. Peter came in a few minutes later, and took only coffee and toast before sitting at the table without so much as a glance in Susannah's direction. The Aunts had spent what was left of the night in the best spare guest chamber, and, since they had not had the forethought to bring pattens to attach to their shoes, Lord Ramsay had promised to drive them back to the Dower House after breakfast.

"And I've been thinking about last night," he continued, making at least two of the persons at the table start guiltily, both of them having done their own share of thinking over the events of those fateful hours before dawn. "I believe the fire might actually have been a good thing, so far as the Ramsay estate is concerned. I wonder if, with the manor house gone, the owner might be persuaded to sell. Peter, I believe the family name is Fairchild, from somewhere in Sussex. Look into it, if you don't mind."

Susannah knew for a fact that Peter would mind very much indeed, but he said only, "Of course, Richard," in a wooden voice and, pushing his plate aside untouched, betook himself from the room.

"You need not do it this instant," Richard protested, but Peter was already halfway through the door. If he heard this admonishment, he paid it no heed.

"Really, Richard!" exclaimed Susannah, disgust in every syllable. "How could you be so cruel?"

"Cruel?" echoed Richard, understandably baffled by this accusation. "All I did was ask him to write to the owner of Fairacres and ask if he would be willing to sell. I daresay he will have no difficulty locating the name and direction; all he need do is look it up in Debrett's."

"Are you really so obtuse?" demanded Susannah,

pushing her own plate away and leaping to her feet to stand over her betrothed and hurl abuses over his head. "When Peter has dreamed of purchasing Fairacres for *years*!"

Richard was suddenly assailed by a multitude of images from last night's fire, most of them involving Peter: Peter standing hip-deep in the river to lay the hose, Peter throwing his weight over and over against one side of the heavy pump. Peter labouring like the humblest peasant in a futile effort to save the house that would never be his. "My dear girl," Richard grumbled, "even if what you say is true, how could I possibly have been expected to know such a thing?"

Susannah was unimpressed with this argument. "I suppose it never would have occurred to you to *ask!* Now I daresay you will expect him to feel honoured to be allowed to administer its lands on your behalf!"

"Well, yes, I will," retorted Richard, goaded beyond endurance. "I pay Peter a very generous wage, so I don't think I am asking too much when I expect him to earn it."

"*Oh!* You are *impossible!*" she ground through clenched teeth, clutching at her unruly curls as if tempted to tear them out by the roots in sheer frustration. Before she could yield to such an impulse, she quitted the room in a cloud of indignation, pausing only long enough to slam the door behind her.

The four people still seated at the table regarded one another in strained silence, until Aunt Charlotte suddenly, and with rare tact, bethought herself of several tasks she needed to complete before returning to the Dower House. She and Aunt Amelia beat a hasty retreat, leaving Richard and Jane in sole possession of the breakfast room.

"Dash it, how was I to know?" Richard demanded of no one in particular. "I can't read the fellow's mind."

"Of course not, Richard," agreed Jane, although her strangled tone and the attention with which she addressed her buttered eggs spoke louder than any words.

"And if he were to tell anyone of his plans, he jolly well ought to have told *me* instead of Susannah," he continued, working himself into a position of righteous indignation. "After all, *I'm* the one who might have been in a position to help him achieve this ambition. But no, he chooses to confide in a slip of a girl with neither connections nor resources, unless we are to count a plantation on the other side of the ocean."

"Perhaps he wanted to accomplish it without your help."

"Am I such an ogre, then, after all I've done for him—paying for his schooling, giving him a home and a position after his education was complete? There's gratitude for you!"

"Perhaps that is the problem," Jane suggested gently. "Gratitude can become a heavy burden, if one has no way of reciprocating."

"Have I ever given any indication that I *wanted* reciprocation?"

"Not that I am aware of, but Peter has his pride, you know." She regarded him with a hint of a smile. "After all, he *is* a Ramsay."

"*Touché,*" said Richard, throwing up a hand to acknowledge this home thrust. "I suppose I had best go and talk to him."

"It would be kindest," she agreed.

He heaved a sigh and pushed his plate away, wondering as he did so if anyone was getting a decent breakfast that day. Just as he had expected, he found Peter in the small chamber that served as his office, writing out a letter in his neat script. On the desk before him, a large volume lay open; Richard would have bet half his inheritance that it was Debrett's.

"Ah, Richard, you were quite right," Peter said, looking up at the entrance of his employer and cousin. "According to Debrett's, Fairacres is the property of one Arthur Edmund Fairchild of Denbury Chase, Sussex."

"Peter," Richard began hesitantly, reaching behind his back to close the door, "Susannah told me you'd had hopes of owning the property yourself someday. Forgive me; I didn't know."

Peter shrugged. "It was nothing but a pipe dream, anyway," he said with an indifference which might have deceived Richard, had he not heard the vociferously expressed truth from his betrothed's lips.

"Still, it is only natural that you should desire a place of your own someday on which to exercise your talents," Richard insisted.

"As to that, I've been thinking." Peter stared with great concentration on the letter before him, but Richard suspected he didn't actually see a word of it. "If you have no objection, I think you should send me to Kentucky, to manage Cousin Susannah's property there."

Richard frowned. "You want to leave England?"

"I think you would be wise to have a man on the property, one who can see at first-hand what it needs, who can administer it and report to you. I understand Susannah's father freed his slaves in his will. That being the case, you will need a man to engage workers to replace those who chose to leave, and to make sure those who remain do not see their new freedom as an excuse to shirk their duties. Who knows?" he asked in a bracing tone. "While I am there, I might be able to acquire a property of my own. I understand land is cheap, if one is willing to put the effort into clearing it."

"Very well, then, if that is what you want," Richard said with obvious reluctance. "I can only say how much I hate the thought of losing you. I shall have the devil of a time finding a steward whose judgment I trust half so well. When would you want to set out?"

"I should prefer to leave at once, if that is possible."

"Surely there is no need for such haste! I had hoped you would stand up with me at my wedding."

"In that case, I should be honoured," Peter said, although a more perceptive man than Richard might have noticed that his voice held nothing but the liveliest dread.

* * *

However vehement her defense of Peter, Susannah had no intention of allowing him to continue to avoid her as he had at breakfast. When he made no appearance at teatime, she had a very good idea of where to look for him. She downed a single cup of tea with uncharacteristic haste, declining to take so much as a single cake from the lavish selection arranged on a plate (a circumstance which in itself would have warned Peter that something was afoot, had he been present to witness it), and excused herself as soon as she could decently do so. She hurried up the stairs to her room, changed her morning gown for her riding habit, and soon descended upon the stables, calling for the groom to saddle Daffodil.

A canter across the fields soon brought her to the property called Fairacres—a property so changed that she hardly would have recognized it, had it not been for the dejected figure of Peter staring bleakly at the pile of charred and blackened timbers from which curls of smoke still rose. She reined in her horse more sharply than she intended, and Daffodil gave a loud snort of protest.

Peter turned at the sound. "Susannah? What are you doing here?"

"Looking for you. When you didn't come to tea, I had a feeling I would find you here."

She lifted her knee over the pommel, and Peter, seeing what she was about, moved mechanically forward to help her dismount. She slid from the saddle and into his arms. As soon as her feet touched the ground, he released his hold on her as if scorched by her touch.

"You shouldn't be here," he protested, glancing back toward the smouldering ruin. "The embers are still hot enough to cause an injury, should you get too close."

"It isn't the embers I want to get close to," she said, taking a tentative step in his direction. "Peter, I know you've been hurt—deeply hurt—but please don't push me away. What happened last night—"

"What happened last night was a mistake," he said in a voice that brooked no argument. "A house burned; a dream died. I was not thinking clearly—it was a moment's madness. It meant nothing."

"It meant something to me," she said softly.

"Susannah, please don't." In spite of his better judgment, he put his hands on her shoulders and gave a little squeeze. "Since you will have it, then yes, it did mean something. It meant a great deal too much, in fact, which is why it must never happen again. You are betrothed to my cousin and employer. Last night, in the heat of the moment—God, what an unfortunate choice of words!—I came dangerously close to forgetting that."

She took a step backward and stared at him. "You intend to let me marry Richard, then, without lifting a finger to stop it?"

"As a man of honour, I can do nothing else," he pointed out, then added gently, "Everything I am and have I owe to Richard. It was he who sent me to university, who gave me a position when my education was complete. I cannot betray him after all he has done for me. You would not want the sort of man who could."

"And what of me, Peter?" she pleaded. "What about me?"

His expression grew wooden, and so did his voice. "As Lady Ramsay, you will of course command my loyalty, just as Richard does."

She stamped her foot and made a little noise of protest rather like an outraged kitten. "What do I care for your loyalty, when I want your lov—"

He put his hand to her mouth to stop the word he dared not speak, or hear spoken, aloud. "Don't say it, Susannah! You know you must not. If I thought for one minute that Richard would mistreat you, if I believed he would be unkind to you, I would stop at nothing to save you from such a marriage. But I know he won't. He will give you no cause to regret marrying him."

"As a wise man once told me, 'the lack of cruelty, even the presence of kindness, is no substitute for—' "

"Surely you cannot mean to compare your lot with that of a slave!" Peter protested, half laughing at the absurdity of hearing his own words thrown back at him in such a context. "As Richard's wife, you will have everything you could possibly wish: a stately home, a high position, an ancient title, a lavish income, clothes, jewels—"

"Oh, everything," Susannah agreed bitterly. "Everything except you. But no, that's wrong, isn't it? I shall have you, too, living under the same roof, my husband's devoted employee. I shall have to see you every day and sit down to dinner with you every night, knowing that my feelings for you are reciprocated, but can never be acted upon. If that is your idea of a brilliant future, I don't think much of it."

"That much, at least, we will be spared," he assured her. "I shall remain at Ramsay Hall for the wedding—I must, for Richard has asked me to attend him at the altar—but immediately afterward, I shall set out for America. I am to administer your property there in Richard's name."

She took a step backwards, and stared at him with stricken blue eyes. "You—you're leaving?"

"Under the circumstances, I think it best." His lips contorted in a travesty of a smile. "It will be a little like being with you, you know, living in the house where you grew up, riding over the acres where you played as a child."

She looked away so that he might not see her rapidly filling eyes. "If you feel that way, I wonder that you are so eager to be rid of me."

"On the contrary, it is the most difficult thing I

have ever done. But as for my being rid of you, Susannah, there is no danger of that. I shall see your face in every hill, in every tree, in every new colt born in the spring, and in every stalk of corn that ripens in summer. You are a part of me, my dear, and I could no more be free of you than I could cut out my own heart."

She was sobbing in earnest now, and he took her in his arms and held her close, knowing all the while that he should not, that every moment they remained thus only served to make the inevitable parting all the more painful. And yet still they stood there, she clinging to him while he murmured words that he could never afterwards quite recall. And if the words sometimes gave way to kisses pressed against her coppery curls, surely he could not be blamed for snatching what crumbs he could as sustenance against the long years of famine that stretched out before him.

17

A mighty pain to love, it is,
And 'tis a pain that pain to miss;
But of all pains, the greatest pain
It is to love, but love in vain.
ABRAHAM COWLEY, *Anacreon*

*I*t was a very subdued Susannah who returned to the house a short time later. As she crossed the hall toward the stairs with her shako in her hand, she was hailed by Jane's voice coming from the direction of the drawing room.

"Susannah, is that you? Thank heaven! I had wondered what had become of you."

"Yes, it's me," Susannah said, accurately if ungrammatically. "I didn't mean to worry you. I—I went riding."

"I can see that from your costume," Jane said, smiling up at her from the sofa, where she sat reading a book with her injured ankle resting on a footstool. "How very becoming that habit looks on you! I knew that shade of bottle green would be just the thing."

"Thank you." Susannah stood awkwardly in the doorway twisting the brim of her hat in her hands. "Was there something you wanted of me?"

"No. Well, that is not quite true. I wanted to tell you that we have heard at last from Monsieur Lavert, the hairdresser from London. He will arrive the day before the ball, so you may surprise us all with your transformation. Antoine has even agreed to give up his own bedchamber to house Monsieur Lavert during his stay—one cannot expect an *artiste* of Monsieur's calibre to put up at a common inn, you know!— although Antoine makes it clear that he is making a great sacrifice. Indeed, I would not have asked such a thing of him, were Monsieur not a fellow countryman in exile."

Susannah's smile was somewhat mechanical. The last thing she wanted to think about at the moment was the betrothal ball—unless, of course, it was the wedding. Hard on the heels of this thought came the recollection of Richard's suggestion that she might wish Jane to attend her at the altar as bridesmaid. The knowledge that Peter would perform a corresponding service for Richard made Jane's presence doubly desirable: Susannah could not bear the thought of the hateful Miss Hunsford making calf's eyes at the man

Susannah loved while she herself plighted her troth to another.

"Oh, that—that is good news," she said with an attempt at brightness. "Actually, there is something I need to discuss with you, as well. The wedding is to be in two weeks' time, you know, and I—I wondered if you would stand up with me. As my bridesmaid."

Lost in her own misery, Susannah did not hear Jane's quick intake of breath, nor did she notice the hand that went instinctively to Jane's bosom as if groping for the hilt of the dagger plunged there.

"I—I should be honoured," Jane said.

Susannah mumbled a word of thanks and then excused herself, pleading the need to change out of her riding habit. Left alone once more, Jane pondered the cruelty of a fate that would allow her to stand at the altar with Richard after all—as attendant to his bride. To her horror, the tears she had held back for so long now welled up in her eyes, and she was powerless to stop them. She fumbled for the handkerchief tucked into her sleeve and sobbed silently into it, her shoulders shaking in quiet misery. And it was here that the Aunts found her when they arrived at Ramsay Hall for dinner.

"Jane!" exclaimed Aunt Amelia, hurrying forward to envelop her in a lavender-scented embrace. "My dear girl, what is the matter?"

"The stupidest thing," Jane said, when she could speak at all. "It is only that, well, we were up so late last night—this morning, really—and I did not sleep well, and have so many things to do before the ball. I am merely tired—nothing that a good night's sleep will not mend. Pay me no heed, I beg you!"

Aunt Amelia patted her hand consolingly. "Forgive me, my dear, but—well, is it the ball, or what the ball represents?"

"It is true that it represents a great deal of work," Jane acknowledged briskly, tucking her sodden handkerchief back into her sleeve. "I must ask Antoine if he will be able to obtain enough lobsters for lobster patties, and I must consult with the gardener regarding the floral arrangements—"

"A great deal of work, to be sure," agreed Aunt Charlotte. "But more than that, it represents Richard's approaching marriage to that American."

"Really, Aunt Charlotte, I wish you would not call her that!" Jane scolded. "Cousin Susannah is very nice girl."

Aunt Charlotte nodded. "A very nice girl whom you would gladly wish at Jericho."

"You need not pretend with us, my dear," Aunt Amelia concurred. "We know how you feel about Richard. Indeed, we have always cherished hopes that someday the two of you might wed."

"Aunt Amelia, you must not talk in such a way! There has never been any question of marriage between Richard and me. I turned down his very generous offer years ago, and he is too much the gentleman to continue to press a suit he knew I did not wish."

"And you were too much the lady to accept a suit you knew *he* did not wish," observed Aunt Charlotte with a great deal too much perspicacity for Jane's peace of mind.

"How I feel for your suffering!" exclaimed Aunt Amelia, groping for her own handkerchief to wipe away her ready tears of sympathy. "I once had an understanding with a young man, you know. But his family's estate was shockingly encumbered, and he was obliged to marry an heiress instead. I was not without other offers—I was accounted quite a beauty in those days, although you would not think it to look at me now—but I could not bear the thought of marriage to another."

In fact, Jane had heard this story many times before, and was not at all surprised when Aunt Amelia begged her pardon and quitted the room, citing the need to collect herself in the light of such painful memories. Aunt Charlotte held her tongue until the door closed behind Aunt Amelia, then turned to Jane.

"Perhaps I haven't Amelia's sensibilities—I never had a proposal of marriage, you know, for I was always far too outspoken to make any man a comfortable wife—but I have often thought Amelia would have been happier if she *had* accepted one of those other offers. There would have been no grand passion, it is true, but it has been my observation that such heights of emotion rarely outlast the honeymoon in any case. In the meantime, she would have had a quiver full of children, and little time to indulge in fantasies of lost love. And now," she concluded, "if you are quite composed, I think you had best change clothes for dinner. We should not like to keep Richard waiting."

"No, indeed," Jane agreed, rising to her feet.

As she changed her day dress for a more formal dinner gown, Jane thought of Aunt Charlotte's words. From that fateful night at dinner when Richard had first announced his betrothal to their American cousin, Jane had told herself that she could be, that she *must* be, happy living at Ramsay Hall as a beloved aunt (although the relationship would actually be a distant cousinship) to Richard's children. Her conversation with the Aunts, however, now caused her to reconsider this prospect. It was true that Aunt Amelia seemed happy enough in spite of her earlier heartbreak, but then again, Aunt Amelia never went to London, and rarely travelled beyond the village of Lower Nettleby; she was not obliged to see her love every day with his new wife, to watch as the other woman's belly grew round with the advent of his heir—a living proof of the intimacy they shared, an intimacy which could never be hers.

Suddenly she knew what she must do. But she would not act rashly; she would give herself time to consider fully the implications of her actions, so that she might make the decision with eyes wide open, never to look back upon it with second guesses or regret. And then, on the night of the betrothal ball, she would at long last accept Sir Matthew Pitney's suit.

18

See golden days, fruitful of golden deeds,
With Joy and Love triumphing.
JOHN MILTON, *Paradise Lost*

The next week passed in a flurry of activity, but it cannot be said that any of the residents of Ramsay Hall enjoyed it. Susannah's dress for the ball was delivered, and the final fittings for her wedding gown scheduled. In addition to her usual household tasks, Jane consulted regularly with the chef and the gardener, and met with the musicians who were hired to play for the ball. Peter booked passage on the merchant ship *Mermaid*, which was to sail from Portsmouth three days after the wedding, and devoted the rest of the week to the task of setting his affairs in order and leaving the estate's books in good condition for his successor. Richard, having no more useful occupation to fill his time, paced restlessly about the house. He had never been taught to be particularly attuned to emotions, either his own or those of others, and was conscious now only of some vague discontent. Having had it drilled into his head from his earliest days that he had a responsibility to his name and his position, he fully intended to do his duty, and expected no less from those around him. To do otherwise would be un—un*English*, and certainly unworthy of a Ramsay of Ramsay Hall. Still, he could not shake the uncomfortable feeling that he was about to make a terrible mistake.

When the day of the ball dawned, the various members of the family hardly knew whether to be sorry or glad. Jane was perhaps the most fortunate, as she was kept busy in the ballroom all the morning, overseeing the footmen as they rearranged the furniture and the gardener's assistants as they placed half a dozen enormous floral arrangements on pillars strategically positioned about the room. In the afternoon, the first of the out-of-town guests began to arrive, and these had to be shown to their rooms and their comfort ensured. As she instructed the housekeeper to show the newest arrivals to the rose bedchamber, Jane consoled herself (if one might call it that) with the knowledge that this would be the last time such a task would fall to her; in another week, such domestic duties would fall within Susannah's purview. As the afternoon progressed, Jane dispatched the groom to the village to meet Monsieur Lavert's arrival on the stage, and to fetch him back to Ramsay Hall in the gig. Finally, after giving Wilson last-minute instructions as to where the musicians were to set up, she climbed the stairs to her own room (leaning rather more heavily on her crutch than had been her wont, as the day's activity had caused her ankle to throb) to dress for the ball.

She did not ring for her maid at once; in truth, she was not quite certain of her ability to control her emotions, and wanted no one to witness any tears she might shed. She opened the clothespress and looked searchingly at the gowns within, giving a rather wistful glance to the mourning gowns she'd worn after the dowager's death. Pushing aside such maudlin thoughts, she removed the cerulean blue ball dress which had been delivered from Madame Lavert's hands earlier that week, Richard having insisted that Jane have a new gown for the occasion. This recollection not unnaturally caused a lump to form in her throat. She swallowed it down, laid the dress gently across the bed, and gave a tug to the bell pull.

When she descended the stairs to the drawing room some time later (having dismissed her maid to assist Miss Ramsay in dressing, once that damsel was released from Monsieur Lavert's hands), she found

Richard and Peter there before her. Richard prowled restlessly about the room, pausing occasionally to rake his fingers through artfully (or perhaps not so artfully) disarranged black locks. Peter stood before the fire, drumming his fingers on the mantel and staring morosely into the blaze.

She gave a little laugh that held a note of hysteria. "It's a ball, you know, not a funeral."

Richard turned to give her a rueful smile in return. "Forgive me, Jane. It is not every day I announce my betrothal."

"I should hope not!" she replied with forced lightness. "It would be very odd if it were."

There was no time for a more extended conversation, for the out-of-town guests began to drift downstairs after completing their own preparations for the ball, and the talk turned to the sort of catching up common to family members who have not seen one another for some time. Then, at last, the door opened once more, and framed in the doorway stood a sight to bring all conversation to a halt.

Susannah was dressed in palest pink gauze over a satin slip of ivory that was surely of no creamier a shade than the rounded bosom that rose and fell over her *décolletage*. Her eyes were wide (and frankly terrified) and her cheeks held the faintest trace of a blush which might have been designed by Nature to coordinate with her gown. More startling than all of this, however, was her hair. The unruly mop of that morning had been ruthlessly sheared, and the short crop which remained had been adorned simply with pearls and allowed to curl as it willed. Indeed, Susannah could not have mussed it if she tried, for—and this was the proof of Monsieur Lavert's genius—it was meant to look mussed. In fact, she looked as if she might have only that moment arisen from her bed—an image that was somehow both innocent and seductive.

Richard, beholding his chosen bride, was conscious of a profound sense of relief, even as he acknowledged that this was hardly an emotion worthy of a man confronting the woman to whom his betrothal was soon to be announced. Uncomfortably aware that his reaction left much to be desired, he moved forward to greet her.

"My dear Cousin Susannah," he said, taking her gloved hand in his, "you have left us all speechless."

She was not quite certain how to interpret this remark. "How do I look?" she asked nervously, her voice hardly more than a whisper.

"Like a baroness," he said, and raised her hand to his lips.

From his vantage point by the fireplace, Peter could not hear this exchange, but he could not fail to notice Susannah's downcast eyes and the rich color that bloomed in her cheeks. He experienced the same sick sensation in the pit of his stomach as he'd felt when he watched Fairacres crash to the ground in a ball of flame.

Soon it was time for the family to take up their positions just inside the ballroom door, where they greeted each new arrival announced by Wilson, thanking the guests for their attendance and presenting them to Miss Ramsay. It was not until half-past nine that they were released from this duty, and Sir Matthew, seeing Jane free at last, lost no time in claiming her hand for the first dance. When the set began to form, however, he made no attempt to lead her onto the floor, but instead asked for the indulgence of a word in private. She knew very well the intent behind this request. At any other time, she would have seized upon her responsibilities as hostess as a convenient excuse to decline it. But Peter had not been the only witness to that exchange between Richard and Susannah, and the sight had only confirmed for Jane the impossibility of continuing at Ramsay Hall, an unwilling intruder upon their wedded bliss. For bliss there would certainly be, and that rather sooner than later; no one who had seen the look in Richard's eyes as he beheld his bride-to-be could doubt it. And so she smiled a bit sadly at Sir Matthew and allowed him to lead her into a small anteroom along one wall.

Once inside this chamber, Sir Matthew lost no time. He closed the door behind them and settled Jane on one of the two straight chairs placed against the wall, where she perched at its edge like a bird poised for flight.

"My dear Miss Hawthorne," he began, taking her hand and dropping to one knee before her, "when I consider the prospect of your being replaced as mistress of Ramsay Hall by that child from America, I can no longer be silent! How I wish to see you installed at Pitney Place as Lady Pitney! How I long to cherish you as you deserve! Do, do say I may!"

"Very well," said Jane, quite steadily. "You may."

Sir Matthew blinked at her, not trusting the evidence of his own ears. "I—I beg your pardon?"

She took a deep breath. "You may install me at Pitney Place as Lady Pitney. You may cherish me as you say I deserve. In short, Sir Matthew, I will marry you."

"My dear Miss Hawthorne—no, my dearest *Jane*!" exclaimed Sir Matthew, overcome with emotion. "I confess, there have been times over the last few years that I feared I should never hear such glorious words fall from your sweet lips! You have made me the happiest of men!"

In proof of this statement, he took her gloved hand and pressed it to his lips; apparently she need not look for passion in her husband—which was, she reflected, probably a good thing.

"But in accepting you, Sir Matthew, I must be honest," she added hastily. "I cannot—I do not feel for you that degree of affection which a man might wish for—indeed, which he ought to expect in his wife. But if you can be content with friendship, then—then I promise I will do all I can to see that you are—are comfortable."

"Pray say no more, my dear Jane! I shall make you learn to love me, and shall revel in the teaching!"

Privately Jane rather doubted her ability to master such a lesson, but since she was quite determined on this course, she held her tongue.

"I shall seek out Lord Ramsay at once," promised Sir Matthew, clambering to his feet. "I know we need not obtain his permission to wed, since you are of legal age, but I am persuaded you should not like to do so without his blessing."

In fact, Jane could think of nothing she would like less than attempting to explain to Richard the sudden reversal in her sentiments where Sir Matthew was concerned. But she could hardly admit such a thing to her newly affianced husband, so she sat numbly on her chair while the blissful bridegroom hurried away in search of his lordship.

He found his quarry just leading Miss Hunsford out of the set as the quadrille ended. "Ah, well met, Lord Ramsay!" he exclaimed gleefully. "How convenient for me that the music should be ending at such an opportune time! I have need of a word alone with you."

Richard glanced about the crowded ballroom. "Can it not wait, Sir Matthew? I should not leave my guests at present."

"I am sure you will forgive my natural impatience when I tell you it concerns Miss Hawthorne."

"Jane?" Richard's brow puckered in a thoughtful frown. "Nothing is wrong, I hope?"

"No, no—quite the reverse, in fact," Sir Matthew assured him. "But I don't like to bandy a lady's name about in public."

Seeing no other way to rid himself of his tiresome neighbor (and, if he were honest with himself, curious to know what Sir Matthew might have to say regarding Jane), Richard consented to grant him five minutes, and led the way out of the ballroom and across the corridor to his study.

"Now, Sir Matthew, I trust you will tell me what this is all about."

"Nothing would give me greater pleasure, my lord. I should like to ask your blessing upon my marriage to your cousin Miss Hawthorne."

Richard shook his head. "God knows I can offer no valid objection to such a match, Sir Matthew, but I fear I can give you no reason to hope for a different answer from Miss Hawthorne than she has given you in the past."

"But that is just what she has done, Lord Ramsay. I have only this moment asked Miss Hawthorne for her hand in marriage, and she has done me the honour of accepting my suit."

"*What?*" The blood seemed to run cold in Richard's veins. A dozen, a hundred images swirled together in his brain: his steadfastness in seeking out Jane whenever he needed a sympathetic ear or an informed opinion; his hope that she might transform Susannah into what he now knew to be a replica of herself; his terror at seeing her fall from the banister; and, finally, his utter revulsion at the thought of her as Sir Matthew's bride. There could be only one conclusion, and one, moreover that he should have reached months—no, years ago. "I don't believe you!" he challenged, with a confidence born of desperation.

Far from being offended by this unflattering response, Sir Matthew chuckled. "I'm sure I don't wonder at it. To be sure, there have been times over the last few years when I wondered if she would ever—but all that is at an end. She has consented to be my wife. I'm sure I need not tell you that I am the happiest of men."

"Where is Jane?" demanded Richard. "I want a word with her. Until I hear from her own lips, I will not—where is she?"

"I left the future Lady Pitney to await my return in one of the antechambers along the west wall—" began Sir Matthew, but soon found himself speaking to the empty air. Lord Ramsay flung himself from the study and back into the ballroom, where he opened the door to each small alcove in turn until he came to the one where Jane sat, pale but composed.

Sir Matthew had caught up to him by this time, and positioned himself beside Jane's chair, placing his hand on her shoulder in a proprietary manner. "Here is Lord Ramsay so surprised he refuses to believe it until he hears it from your own fair lips," he told her with a self-satisfied smile. "But he assures me he can have no objection to the match, so you need have no fears on that head, my love."

"Is it true, Jane?" demanded Richard. "Have you agreed to marry Sir Matthew?"

"Yes," she said baldly.

Sir Matthew patted her shoulder and once again proclaimed himself the happiest of men.

"Yes, well, I should like to have a word alone with my cousin, Sir Matthew," Richard said. "Until I am convinced that she considers herself the happiest of women, I cannot give my consent."

"Your consent is not necessary, Richard," Jane pointed out. "Recall that I have been of legal age for the last eight years and more."

"But still as lovely as you were when you first came to Ramsay Hall as a girl of eighteen," Sir Matthew assured her in ardent tones.

Richard neither confirmed nor denied this assessment of Jane's charms, but strode to the door and held it open pointedly. "If you will excuse us, Sir Matthew?"

"Very well, my lord." To Jane, he added, "I shall leave you to persuade Lord Ramsay of the strength of my devotion."

In full confidence of this happy outcome, he took his leave. Richard closed the door after him and turned on Jane. "Of the strength of Sir Matthew's devotion I have no need of persuasion, for he has plagued you with it for the better part of a decade. Yours, however, I beg leave to doubt. Jane, how could you?"

"How could I what?"

"Do not play the dunce with me, my girl! How could you accept Sir Matthew's proposal when I know full well that you can barely tolerate the man?" His eyes narrowed in sudden suspicion. "Has that idiot been filling your head with nonsense about your being no longer welcome at Ramsay Hall? If he has, by God, I'll—"

"He has done no such thing," Jane insisted, coming to her betrothed's defense. "Oh, I do not deny your approaching nuptials influenced my decision, but Sir Matthew has not said anything that had not occurred to me on my own."

"And the—how did your affianced husband put it?—the 'strength of your devotion' toward him?"

To her annoyance, Jane felt her face grow warm, and knew she was blushing. "I assure you, I never gave Sir Matthew any reason to suppose—in fact, I told him quite plainly that I—that I do not feel for him that degree of affection that a man might hope to inspire in his wife. If he is not troubled by its absence, I see no reason why you should be."

"And what of you?"

He took a rather menacing step in her direction, and Jane leaned back in her chair in an attempt to put as much distance between them as possible. "What—what about me?"

He took another step closer, and she found herself cowering against the back of her chair like a cornered animal.

"There was a time when you had strong feelings on the subject of making a loveless marriage."

She knew he was thinking of her rejection of his own long-ago proposal, and hurried into speech to cover her embarrassment. "On the contrary, I believe a loveless marriage may be quite happy, so long as there is mutual respect and friendship. But a marriage where love is on one side only—" She broke off abruptly, horribly aware of having said too much.

"I see," Richard said slowly, regarding her with piercing dark eyes. "How long have you known?"

There was no point in denying it. "I knew it from the first," she confessed.

He stared at her. "But that is impossible!"

"Believe me," she said ruefully, "it is not."

"But I have only just discovered it myself!" he exclaimed, recalling that horrific moment in his study when he'd learned that Jane, *his* Jane, had betrothed herself to a man who was not worthy to tie her bootlaces.

"Permit me to point out that I am rather more closely concerned in the matter," she said with a sad little smile.

"I should like to know how you arrived at that conclusion! You may say I have been remarkably obtuse, but I maintain that no one can be more closely concerned in the matter of my feelings than I am."

"Richard, what *are* you talking about?" she asked, baffled by this seeming *non sequitur*.

"I am saying I love you, dammit!" he shouted. "And although I might stand aside for a better man, I will not permit you to marry that bore, Sir Matthew Pitney!"

In proof of this statement, he grabbed her by the arms, lifted her bodily from her chair, and kissed her in a manner that left her in no doubt as to the violence of his affections.

"Oh Richard, Richard!" she said in between kisses, laughing and crying at the same time. "You dear, dense man, don't you know I've loved you from the first?"

"And yet you rejected my proposal," he reminded her.

"Only because you so clearly did *not* want to make it! Loving you as I did, how could I put my wishes ahead of your own?"

"Promise me you won't marry Sir Matthew!"

"No, no, of course I won't! Indeed, I never really wanted to, but I could not bear to live here and see you married to Cousin Susannah!"

He snapped his fingers. "*That* for Cousin Susannah! I would not allow you to marry Sir Matthew were I a hundred times married to her!"

Jane could find nothing to dispute in these sentiments, but the recollection of Richard's betrothal was sufficient to wipe the smile from her face, and she exclaimed with dismay, "But Richard, you cannot have thought! Your betrothal is to be announced within the hour!"

"No, it is not—not anymore."

"You cannot *jilt* the poor girl!"

"I can, and I will. I shall assuage my conscience with the knowledge that she has no more desire to marry me than I have to marry her." In a more serious tone, he added, "I have spent my entire life putting my duty ahead of my own inclinations—indeed, I was raised to believe I had an obligation to do so. But not now, not this time. My future happiness, and yours, is too important to throw away for the sake of mere propriety."

" 'Mere' propriety, Richard?" Her voice was faintly mocking, but her face was radiant with happiness. "This, from you? If I had any doubts as to your sentiments, they are surely answered."

"My dearest love!"

He took her in his arms (more gently this time) and

kissed her quite thoroughly, and their kisses were all the sweeter for having been so long deferred. Alas, the sound of the anteroom door opening caused them to jump apart. Sir Matthew Pitney stood in the doorway, the picture of outraged virtue.

"My lord! Have the goodness to unhand my fiancée!"

"Go to the devil," recommended Richard.

"You think to insult me in addition to manhandling the woman who is to become my wife? I will have satisfaction, sir! My second will wait upon you in the morning!"

"No, no, you quite misunderstand the matter," Jane said soothingly, in an attempt to pour oil over troubled waters. "I am very sorry, Sir Matthew, but I cannot marry you, after all. It is Lord Ramsay, you see. I— he—"

"Oh, yes, I see very well!" declared Sir Matthew, fairly quivering with indignation. "I wonder what Miss Ramsay would say to the information that her betrothed is having a bit of slap-and-tickle with the former companion of his sainted mother?"

He quitted the little room without waiting for an answer, and if he resisted the urge to slam the door, there was no denying that he shut it with a disapproving "click." Richard and Jane stared silently at the space he had vacated, until Jane found her tongue at last.

"Oh, dear! He is quite right, you know; that is exactly how it will be perceived, once it becomes known that we—"

"Yes, and that is why we must marry as soon as may be arranged. In the meantime, you will remove to the Dower House as soon as our guests depart, and will remain there with the Aunts until the wedding. I will not have it said that there has been anything in the least salacious about your presence in this house since Mama's death!"

"No, not that," Jane said impatiently. "That is, of course I will marry you whenever you wish. But Cousin Susannah must certainly be told before—"

As if on cue, the door opened once more, and Susannah tripped lightly into the room. "Richard, Sir Matthew says—" She broke off abruptly, and her eyes grew round at the sight of Richard and Jane, their newfound happiness obvious in spite of the guilt writ large upon their faces. "So it's true, then!"

"Susannah—" With some reluctance, Richard released Jane and stepped forward. "My dear girl, I am sorrier than I can say—"

"Nonsense!" Susannah declared briskly. "You never gave me any reason to believe that you loved me—in fact, I have often wondered why you didn't marry Cousin Jane years ago, for it is obvious that you were meant for each other!"

"Excellent creature!" declared Richard, taking Susannah's hand and raising it to his lips.

"I am only sorry you were put to the trouble and expense of my passage from America." She glanced at Jane. "I'm sorry, too, that I never did learn to behave like a proper lady."

Richard was moved to protest this self-denigration. "Now, *that* I cannot regret, for had you not arrived and set us all on our ears, God only knows how long I might have continued in ignorance of my own heart. Since the betrothal has not been formally announced, I trust that any embarrassment to you will be minimal. If anyone dares to say anything, we will merely express astonishment that our American cousin's visit could be so misconstrued. In the meantime, I will make it up to you, Susannah, I promise. Next spring Jane and I will sponsor you for a Season in London, and you will have the most brilliant come-out any young lady ever had: presentation at Court, vouchers for Almack's—"

"I'm afraid that won't be possible."

Three heads turned toward the door, which had opened once more to admit yet another person into the tiny room which was by now becoming quite crowded.

"Susannah will not be here next spring," Peter

explained. "She will be returning to America on the *Mermaid*."

"Will she?" Jane asked doubtfully. "You need not, Susannah, if you do not wish it. In any case, I'm not at all certain we can find a woman to accompany you on such short notice."

"No woman will be necessary," Peter said.

Richard looked down at his erstwhile betrothed in some consternation. "You cannot make such a journey alone!"

"I quite agree," Peter said, moving forward to slip his arm about her waist. "Fortunately, she will not be travelling alone. She will be returning to America as Mrs. Peter Ramsay."

"Oh, Peter!" Susannah squealed, throwing her arms about his neck.

He received her with great willingness, and although they did not so far forget themselves as to kiss in full view of two other people, their embrace left neither of the spectators in any doubt as to their sentiments.

"Peter Ramsay!" Richard regarded his steward with mock indignation. "I accused you once of trying to steal a march on me. It appears I was closer to the truth than I knew!"

"Yes," Peter said, detaching himself with some

reluctance from Susannah's arms, "but it was not my intention, I assure you. It just, well, it just *happened*. I did not mean to—I am sorry if—"

"You need not apologize," Richard assured him. "Unless, of course, it is to Miss Hunsford. I believe she had her hopes quite set on you."

"I could almost feel sorry for that horrid Miss Hunsford," Susannah said, brushing traces of her rice powder from Peter's hitherto immaculate cravat with a proprietary air. "Almost, but not quite."

"Perhaps she and Sir Matthew can console one another," Richard suggested to Jane, his newfound happiness finding expression in absurdity.

Beyond the closed door, the violins ground to a halt, and a gong sounded—the cue for everyone to locate his or her partner for supper, and the prearranged signal for the betrothal announcement that was to precede the meal.

"Oh, my!" exclaimed Jane. "Everyone was told to expect an announcement!"

"And an announcement they shall have," Richard said, taking her hand. "Two, in fact. Peter, Susannah, are you coming?"

Susannah would have followed him, but Peter grabbed her wrist. "We'll be there directly," he said. "We have unfinished business to attend."

Richard gave the pair a knowing look. "Don't be too long. It's shockingly bad form, you know, missing your own engagement announcement," he said, then drew Jane's hand through his arm and sallied forth to do the honours.

About the Author

At the age of sixteen, Sheri Cobb South discovered Georgette Heyer, and came to the startling realization that she had been born into the wrong century. Although she doubtless would have been a chambermaid had she actually lived in Regency England, that didn't stop her from fantasizing about waltzing the night away in the arms of a handsome, wealthy, and titled gentleman.

Since Georgette Heyer was dead and could not write any more Regencies, Ms. South came to the conclusion she would simply have to do it herself. In addition to her popular series of Regency mysteries featuring idealistic young Bow Street Runner John Pickett (described by *All About Romance* as "a little young, but wholly delectable"), she is the award-winning author of several Regency romances, including the critically acclaimed *The Weaver Takes a Wife*.

A native and long-time resident of Alabama, Ms. South recently moved to Loveland, Colorado, where she has a stunning view of Long's Peak from her office window.

Made in the USA
Middletown, DE
11 February 2019